HE FELT THE THRILL OF PURSUIT. THE INSTINCTS OF A KILLER HAD BECOME HIS OWN.

Newman began to run after Karl. He had closed the gap. He felt stronger, as if he could run on at this pace until he grew old and died. Karl steadied himself and aimed the .45 with both hands. He heard another click as Karl squeezed the trigger in a kind of blind panic.

Newman laughed loudly and Karl heard him; it was an explosion of mirthless and savage sound.

"It's empty, you son of a bitch. . . . It's empty and I'm coming!"

"ONE BURNS WITH SYMPATHY FOR THEIR PURSUIT OF JUSTICE, HOWEVER ONE MAY BE CHILLED BY THEIR METHODS."   —*The Boston Globe*

WILDERNESS

ROBERT B. PARKER

A DELL BOOK

A SEYMOUR LAWRENCE BOOK

Published by
Dell Publishing
a division of
Bantam Doubleday Dell Publishing Group, Inc.
666 Fifth Avenue
New York, New York 10103

ISBN: 0-440-19328-1

Reprinted by arrangement with Delacorte Press/Seymour Lawrence.

Printed in the United States of America

One previous Dell edition

New Dell edition

October 1983

20 19 18 17 16 15 14 13 12

RAD

*This is for Joan in whom
God finally got it right.*

WILDERNESS

Prologue

It was Wednesday and the sky was a flat acrylic blue when Aaron Newman saw the murder. He was jogging home from the health club along the railroad tracks. His biceps were pumped up from forty-five curls, his pectorals swollen from forty-five bench presses, his latissimus dorsi engorged from forty-five pull downs. His legs felt loose and easy and the sweat seemed to oil the hinges of his body as he ran. His breathing was easy and spring was still left in his calves. Ahead of him, where the road looped in close to the tracks, he saw a tall gaunt man with black hair slicked back fire three shots into the head of a kneeling woman. The gun was short and gray, and after the third shot the man slipped it under his coat and got into a blue Lincoln with an orange vinyl roof and drove away.

The woods were still. There was a locust hum and a bird chatter that Newman didn't recognize. He stood where he had stopped and looked at the woman's body. He was too far to see clearly, but the back of her head was bloody and she was motionless, lying on her side, her knees bent. She looked like a small animal that had been run over on the road. Newman was sure she was dead.

"Jesus Christ," he said.

He began to walk toward her slowly, squinting, fuzzing his vision deliberately so that he didn't have to see the scramble of brains and blood. A crow swooped in from his left and landed on the ground beside the woman's body with a rustle of wings. Newman jumped at the sudden dark flash of life. The bird pecked at the pulpy mass of the woman's head and Newman looked away.

"Jesus Christ," he said. He picked up a pine cone and threw it at the crow; it flared up away from the woman and circled into a tree.

"Nevermore," Newman said.

He stood now directly over the woman, squinting, looking only obliquely at her. He didn't want to touch her. What if he touched her and she were alive with her brains drooling out of the back of her head. If she moved he was afraid he'd bolt. He felt helpless. He wouldn't be able to help her. He'd better run for the cops. It was maybe another mile. That wasn't hard. He'd run thirteen Friday. He'd already run nine today.

Is she dead? they'd say.

I don't know, I didn't dare touch her, he'd say.

And the cops would look at each other. No, it would be too embarrassing. He'd have to touch her. He squatted down on his heels and felt around for her neck, looking at her only sideways with his eyes nearly shut. He felt for the pulse in the carotid artery. The same place he took his own after running. There was no pulse. He made himself feel hard for nearly a minute. Nothing. As he moved his hand he felt something warm and wet and jerked his hand away and rubbed it on the ground without looking. He stood up. The woods were nearly all white pine here, and the sun coming through the trees made a ragged dappled pattern on the woman's white slacks. One shoe was missing. Her toenails were painted maroon.

Newman turned and began to jog down the railroad tracks. As he jogged he could feel the panic build in him, and he ran faster toward the cops.

1

She was there when he drove back with the two local cops. The crows had been at her, and as the patrol car pulled in beside the railroad tracks three crows flew up and went to the trees.

For the two cops it was the first shooting victim they had ever seen. They had seen bad corpses in car wrecks and people who'd died of heart attacks on the way to the hospital, and once they'd had to remove the remains of an old man who had died three weeks prior. But never before a murder. The murder scared them a little.

The senior officer was Ed Diamond, six and a half years on the force. Four years of high school, three years in the Army and on the cops. He was not quite twenty-eight.

"Check her, Jim," he said.

Jimmy Tinkham was twenty-six, high school, college, a criminal justice major, and onto the Smithfield force. He was blond. His cheeks were rosy and he shaved three times a week.

He squatted beside her, the big handle of his service revolver sticking out at an odd angle. He felt her neck as Newman had done. Newman liked that. He'd been professional. Like they were.

"Dead and starting to cool," Tinkham said.

Diamond nodded. "I figured," he said. Above them on the tree branch in a row, the crows sat. Their bodies motionless, moving their heads.

"We better run it through," Tinkham said.

Diamond nodded. He took a notebook from his shirt pocket, a pencil from the same pocket. He pushed his campaign hat back on his head a bit more; the Smithfield force wore them in the summer.

"What time you find her?" he said.

Newman shrugged. "I don't know," he said. "I left the health club at five. It's about four miles to here. I run ten-minute miles. It must have been about twenty of six."

Diamond wrote 5:40 in his notebook. "She just the way you left her?"

"Yes."

"And you saw the man shoot her?"

"Yes."

"Why didn't you intervene?"

"It was too quick. I was too far away. It was over before I knew what happened."

"And you didn't get the license number?"

"469—AAG," Newman said. He hadn't consciously registered it. It surprised him. But he knew that he noticed things. He always had.

Tinkham raised his eyebrows and stuck out his lower lip.

Diamond said, "Can you give us a description?"

"Of him or the car?" Newman said.

"Both. Him first."

"He was tall. Maybe six three, and skinny. No, not

skinny, gaunt, but sort of strong looking, like Lincoln, you know?"

Diamond wrote 6'3". *Lean. Muscular.*

"And his hair was black and slicked back tight against his scalp. Short. No sideburns. He had on a lime green leisure suit and white shiny loafers with brass tassels."

"And the car?"

"Lincoln, new. Orange roof, blue body. Roof is vinyl." Newman found himself talking like a television cop. *Christ,* he thought, *even here I'm trying to sound right.*

"Okay," Diamond said, "now where were you . . ."

"Eddie," Tinkham said. "Why fuck around with that? You know the staties are going to do this and we're not. We don't even have mug books, for crissake. Whyn't you put out a pick-up on the radio for that car with that description. Then we'll inventory the scene so that when some state police corporal shows up here and looks around he won't think we're a couple of fucking assholes."

Diamond nodded and went to the patrol car.

"Aren't you the writer?" Tinkham said.

Newman nodded. "The one," he said.

"Oughta get a few good stories out of this one," Tinkham said.

Newman nodded.

"I see you running every day," Tinkham said. He stood with his back to the dead woman. The earth had rotated a bit and the dappling shadow of the trees fell across the police cruiser, leaving the woman in shade. "How far you go?"

"I do about ten miles," Newman said. "Three days a week I run up to the health club and lift a little."

"Losing any weight?" Tinkham said.

"Yeah. Maybe twenty, twenty-five pounds so far," Newman said. He was conscious of saying *yeah*. A regular guy. One of the boys. At ease with cops and jocks and guys that played pool for money.

One of the crows made a swoop over the dead woman and didn't dare. He kept in the air and circled back up to the tree branch. There were five crows there now.

Diamond came back from the cruiser. "Couple of staties coming down from the Smithfield barracks," he said. "Alden says don't touch anything till they get here."

Tinkham nodded. "You want to write?" he said.

Diamond said, "Yes."

Tinkham squatted down again beside the woman. "Female," he said. "Black, age"—he shrugged—"twenty to thirty, white slacks, yellow halter top, black sling-strap high-heel shoe (one), one shoe missing, gold hoop earrings."

Diamond said, "You sure there's two?"

"You want to turn her head and look?" Tinkham said.

Diamond said "No" and continued to write in his notebook.

"Large gold ring on index finger of right hand, picture of a queen on it."

Diamond said, "What?"

"Picture of a queen," Tinkham said. "How the fuck do I know who it is. You know?" He looked at Newman.

Newman leaned closer. *You get used to anything.* The woman's hand was sprawled out away from her body and Newman could look at the ring without seeing the shattered skull.

"Nefertiti," he said.

Diamond looked at him. Tinkham said, "Or at least not often."

"It's the King Tut craze," Newman said.

Diamond said, "Never mind."

"Victim is prostrate on left side, appears to have been shot several times in right rear quarter of head. No evidence of rape or sexual abuse. No sign of struggle. No bruises or abrasions on visible parts of body, neck, right arm. Face obscured by blood and disfigured by apparent gunshot wound."

Newman realized he'd been hearing the siren for a time without noticing. Then a blue Massachusetts State Police car pulled in beside the Smithfield cruiser. Behind it, another Smithfield cruiser.

"Inside of the right arm shows marks of probable hypodermic injections," Tinkham said.

Two big troopers got out of the Massachusetts State Police car. They wore campaign hats and black boots. Their faces glistened with the closeness of their shaves. Their uniform shirts were pressed with military creases. Their gunbelts glowed with polish. Their hair barely showed under the hats. The sideburns were trimmed short. One was black.

The white trooper said to Diamond, "Touch anything?"

Diamond shook his head.

The black trooper looked down at the woman. "Black," he said. "What the hell she doing out here?"

Tinkham said, "I don't know. She don't live around here, though."

The black trooper looked at Tinkham for ten seconds, then he said, "No shit?"

Tinkham's face reddened. "Maybe she was selling watermelon," he said.

The black trooper smiled. Once. A smile that came on and went off. He looked down at the woman. "Junkie," he said.

The white trooper said, "Tracks?"

The black trooper nodded. "All up and down her right arm."

The white trooper said to Newman, "You see the shooting?"

"Yes," Newman said.

"Could you identify the killer?"

"Yes," Newman said. "I'm sure I could."

2

It's like the Army, Newman thought. *You go in one end of the process and it starts taking you along and you get numb and after a while you come out the other end. Honorable discharge. Or whatever.* He sat at a gray metal table in the homicide squadroom at state police headquarters on Commonwealth Avenue and looked at the pictures of criminals in large albums. He was still in warm-up pants and a white T-shirt that said Adidas across the front. He wore yellow Nike training shoes with a blue swoosh. The sweat that had been so lubricant two hours earlier had stiffened and chilled. He was hungry.

At 8:47 in the evening he saw the man. Profile and full face, staring at him. Hair slicked back, deep eye sockets. Adolph Karl, male, Caucasian, dob 7/15/30, aka Addie Kaye.

"This is him," Newman said.

A state police detective named Bobby Croft swung his feet down off the top of his desk and walked over. He looked at Karl's picture.

"Him?" Croft said. "Adolph Karl? Son of a bitch. You sure?"

Newman said, "Yes. That's him. I'm sure."

Croft walked to the end of the squadroom, opened the frosted glass half-door that said Lieutenant Vincent on it, and poked his head inside.

"Hey, Murray," he said. "Come have a look."

Lieutenant Vincent came out, round-faced and graceful, with a bald head and blue-rimmed glasses. He walked down to the table where Newman sat and looked over Newman's shoulder at the mug book.

"Show him," Croft said.

Newman pointed to the picture of Adolph Karl. "Him," he said.

Vincent raised his eyebrows and looked at Croft. He said to Newman, "You're sure?"

"I'm sure," Newman said.

Vincent smiled. "Why don't you have Adolph brought in, Bobby. We can put him in a show-up and just double check. We wouldn't want Adolph's civil rights compromised."

Croft nodded and went out of the squadroom.

Newman said, "You know this Karl, Lieutenant?"

Vincent said, "Yes. He's a bad man. Prostitution, narcotics, loan sharking, extortion. He's important enough to have most of his assaults done for him now. I'm a little surprised. Must have been personal. Anybody with him in the car?"

"There must have been," Newman said. "He got in the passenger's side when the car drove off."

"And he did it himself." Vincent sucked on his bottom lip. "You want some coffee?"

Newman nodded.

Vincent said to a uniformed trooper, "Charlie, get us a cup of coffee, will you? Cream and sugar?"

Newman said, "Black."

Vincent went back to his office.

The trooper brought the coffee. "You want more," he said, "out that door and turn right."

Newman said, "Thanks."

He drank the coffee and three more cups. He read the morning paper. He looked at the policemen coming and going. He stared at the fluorescent lights. At a quarter to twelve Croft came into the squadroom.

"Let's take a look, Mr. Newman."

The show-up room was dark. Three men stood on a small lighted stage. One of them was Adolph Karl. He was wearing a dark blue polyester leisure suit with light blue piping, and a light blue polyester shirt with dark blue trim. His hair was black and combed tightly against his skull. It looked wet. His eyes were deep in the eye sockets. His ears stuck out. He swallowed once and his big Adam's apple moved. Newman knew that Karl couldn't see him in the dark, but he felt scared. Six hours earlier Newman had seen Karl shoot the back of a woman's head off.

"Recognize the murderer among those men?" Croft said.

"On the end in the blue leisure suit. That's him."

Croft said, "You're sure?"

Newman nodded, then realized Croft couldn't see him in the dark. "Yes," he said. "I'm sure."

"No doubts? You could swear to it in court?"

"Yes."

"All right," Croft said. He stressed the second word. They went out of the show-up room and back to Croft's desk. Lieutenant Vincent came out of his office. Croft nodded at him. Three times.

Vincent smiled. "Very good," he said. "His lawyer with him?"

Croft said, "Yeah, but we got the son of a bitch, Murray. Lawyer or no lawyer."

Vincent said, "If he sticks." He nodded at Newman.

Newman said, "I'll stick, I'm sure it's him. I saw him."

Vincent smiled. "Sure. I know you will. And it's a damned good thing to bag Karl. We've wanted him for a long time."

"What happens now?" Newman said.

"We'll process Karl. There will be a preliminary hearing. We'll let you know. Eventually we'll go to court and you'll testify."

"Can I leave now?"

"Yeah, but first a man from the Essex County DA's office wants a statement."

"They bring you in in the cruiser?"

"Yes."

"Bobby," Vincent said. "When he's through, whyn't you run Mr. Newman up to wherever it is."

"Smithfield," Newman said.

"Yeah, Smithfield. Whyn't you run Newman up to Smithfield. When you come back, come in and we'll chat."

Croft nodded.

It was nearly 2 A.M. when they went north up Route 93. Newman said to Croft, "What did the lieutenant mean, 'If he sticks'?"

The police radio was a soft murmur in the background, so low Newman wondered how Croft could hear it.

Croft shrugged in the dark. "People change their minds sometimes. Decide they made a mistake. An eyewitness is good at the beginning but a lot better at the end."

"I didn't make a mistake," Newman said.

Croft was silent. The radio murmured. The dispatcher's voice rhythmic and without affect. The messages indistinguishable to Newman.

Croft glanced over at Newman, then looked back at the road.

Newman was exhausted. He'd been up since six-thirty. The coffee he'd drunk made him jumpy but no less tired. It felt corrosive in his stomach. He leaned his head back against the headrest and took a deep breath. *Forty-six*, he thought. *I'm forty-six years old.*

Croft turned off at Route 128. "Mr. Newman," he said, "I'm going to say something that Lieutenant Vincent would cut off my balls for saying."

Newman opened his eyes and rolled his head over and looked at Croft.

"The reason we're wondering if you'll stick is because we're wondering if someone might squeeze you. You got a right to know what you're getting into, and Adolph Karl is a fucking psychopath."

A thrill of fright flickered in Newman's stomach.

"You mean he might try to stop me from testifying."

"Yeah."

"Would he kill me?"

"I think he'd threaten you first. We can give you protection. It ain't all that bad. But it may be awkward for a while."

"How long would I have to have protection?"

"Hard to say," Croft answered. "We don't have to worry about it now. Nobody knows who you are."

"But at the hearing?"

"Then they'll know. Then we'll cover you. It'll be all right, but I figure you got the right to know how it'll work. And the sooner you know, the longer you'll have to get used to it."

The car pulled off 128 at the Main St.–Smithfield exit. It was twenty minutes of three and the streets were empty.

"Where to from here?" Croft said.

"Keep going straight. I'll tell you." The thrill of fright vibrated steadily now in Newman's stomach. He could feel the electric buzz of it in his fingertips and along the insides of his arms.

3

The house was dark when he went in the kitchen. Janet would be in bed. She was not a waiter-up. He switched on the light and looked at the kitchen clock: 2:50. He got a can of Miller beer out of the refrigerator and opened it and turned off the kitchen light and sat at the kitchen table and sipped the beer. The outside spotlights were on, and he looked at the roll of his lawn back up to the big white pines that marked the end of his lawn and the beginning of Chris Hood's. The house was still. He looked at the paneled walls of the kitchen and the copper stove-hood and the chop-block counters. Janet had planned it all. And what she made was beautiful always. The house was two hundred years old and she was careful to keep the sense of age even in a modern kitchen. He got up and got another beer. The tingle of panic that he'd felt since Croft had spoken of reprisal had faded. He felt strong and calm in this house, looking out of the darkened room at the lighted green lawn.

He'd do what he must. A man had to do that. He laughed a little to himself. *Sound like someone doing a parody of my novels.* There was no shame in the fear. But there was shame, he thought, if you let the fear control you. *I'll do what I must.* And the police would protect them. He drank some of the beer. He was tired but he no longer felt jittery. The coffee seemed to have lost its sting. *Janet won't be too thrilled with a bodyguard. Explain that one to the folks in the department, lovey.* He smiled again to himself in the dark, finished the beer. *One more can.* He imagined his wife giving her course in sexual stereotyping while a swag-bellied cop in a Sam Browne belt and black holster leaned against the door frame. *She'll be pissed.*

But you couldn't let some guy shoot a woman and walk away. A man couldn't do that. "Christ, she doesn't even know," he said aloud. She gave a graduate seminar every Tuesday evening. She probably hadn't gotten home till ten. His note had simply said *In Boston, back late.* He hadn't wanted her to worry and it was too complicated to explain in a note. He drank beer. There was half a can left.

He hated to be out when she came home. He loved to see her come home from work. She dressed so well. Her makeup was so perfect. She was so in charge with her black briefcase and her tailored clothes and her hair in perfect order. She always looked so beautiful that he wanted to make love with her on the couch with her clothes still on in an explosion of affection and desire. He never did, though. She never wanted to. Always had to be when she said, and under her circumstances. *Control. She's always gotta be in control.* Always it was at night when she didn't have to wash her hair. Never when she had an early class. Always after a bath. Never if her good clothes would wrinkle. Always she touched him. Never he touched her. Always she ended the foreplay. *Still, it's regular. You can count on it.* He finished the beer. *No point running over that dead trail again. Nothing's perfect. We're doing fine.*

He put the three empty beer cans in the kitchen wastebasket, went to the downstairs bathroom to urinate, and headed up to bed.

The bedroom was dark when he went in. The airconditioner was on. He closed the door behind him. Janet made a muffled noise on the bed and moved. The noise was something like a groan. She made it again. The thrill of fear surged back. His face felt hot. He turned on the overhead light.

"Oh my Jesus Christ," he said.

His wife was lying naked on top of the bed. Her ankles were bound together with clothesline and so were her knees. Her hands were tied behind her back. Three loops of clothesline pinned her upper arms against her body. Her underpants had been wadded tightly and wedged into her mouth. One leg of her panty hose had been ripped off and used to hold the gag in place. The length of tan nylon was very thin where it held the wadded cloth in her mouth, and wider at the corners of her mouth and across her cheeks to where it had been knotted behind her neck. Her eyes were wide and tearful but she looked more angry than frightened. On her stomach, just above the line of her pubic hair, someone had scratched AK with a sharp point. The scratches were shallow. The gag forced her mouth slightly open, and Newman noticed that the wadded underpants had a floral pattern.

She groaned at him again, insistently, and her eyes were as wide as she could make them. She shrugged her body angrily on the bed. For a moment he stood soundless and without motion. The panic that flooded over him gave way to an urge to rape her. There she was. Miss Complete Control, absolutely helpless for the first time since he'd known her. She couldn't turn away. She couldn't even talk. The two impulses flushed his face and paralyzed him for a moment. Then he thought of who might have done it. AK. He reached behind the bedroom door and took the double-barreled 12-gauge shotgun he always kept there. From the ledge above the door he took two shells, broke the shotgun, put in the shells, and snapped the gun closed.

She made a series of grunting sounds at him through the gag. He cocked both hammers. Holding the shotgun in his right hand he sat on the edge of the bed and, with his left hand, he fumbled the length of panty hose from her mouth, slipping it down over her chin. He took the gag from her mouth. It was soaked with saliva. He kept his eyes on the door.

"Ahhhh," she said. "Ah, ah ah." It wasn't crying. Exactly. Her breath shook as she dragged it in. "They're gone, you sonova bitch, untie me. Bastard, sonova bitch. Fucking bastard untie me."

"Who . . . ?" he said.

"Untie me you bastard bitch fucking bastard untie me."

She kicked her bound feet up and down, banging her helpless heels on the bed in a frenzy of frustration.

"Okay," he said. "Okay, hold still." He slid the bolt on the bedroom door. They'd put it there so the kids wouldn't come in and catch them making love. Now the kids were gone and they usually didn't need it.

"Will you untie me you bitch master."

He took a jackknife from his pocket and sawed through the ropes that held her. Cutting always with the blade edge away from her. He did it all with his left hand. In his right he still held the shotgun.

She sat up on the bed, her knees drawn up, her hands crossed across her breasts, her shoulders bent forward, her head almost touching her knees. She inhaled. Her breath went in long trembling gasps. He shifted the shotgun to his left hand and put his arm around her. She pulled away, then scrambled off the bed and went to the closet. She took out an ankle-length green robe and put it on and zipped it up.

Standing at the foot of the bed she looked at him as he sat with the shotgun held up, barrel toward the ceiling, both barrels cocked.

"They were here when I came home," she said. "I came home from my class and came in the kitchen door and put my briefcase on the table and there they were. Two of them. They had guns and one of them had clothesline coiled up, with the paper label still around it, right like it comes from the store. And I said 'What the hell are you doing here,' and they took hold of me and pushed me down on the floor and one of them tied my hands behind me and the other one undressed me. I tried to scream but the first one put his hand over my mouth, and then they gagged me and made me walk upstairs with no clothes on and they put me on the bed and tied me up the rest of the way, and then the one who had the rope took his jackknife and scratched my stomach with it and they left."

"Did they say anything?"

She shivered. Her arms were folded tight across her chest and her shoulders hunched. He wanted to put his arms around her and have her bury her face in his shoulder and cry, and he wanted to say *There there it's all right. I'm here. Go ahead and cry it out.* But he knew if he reached for her she'd shrink away.

"No. It was awful. Neither one ever said a word. Not to me. Not to each other."

"I'm sorry I wasn't here."

She shrugged. "They had guns. You'd have ended up beside me."

"Maybe," he said. "The sons of bitches. I'll kill them if I can."

She smiled very faintly.

The phone rang. They both looked automatically at the clock. Four fifteen. It rang again. With the shotgun pointing toward the floor, the hammers still cocked, he stepped to the bedside table on her side where the phone sat. He picked it up with his left hand.

"Hello?"

"You find her yet?" The voice was uneducated, flattened by a Boston accent.

"Find who?"

"Your old lady. The bimbo we left done up like a wet wash in the bedroom."

The fear wasn't a sudden stab anymore. It was a steady hurt that waxed and waned but never vanished. Now it was powerful and he felt weak from it.

"Yeah, I found her," he said.

"See the initials above her snatch?"

Newman nodded.

"Did you?" The voice was harsher.

"Yes. I saw them." He squeezed his hand around the smooth stock of the shotgun where it narrowed at the breech. What if they came and it wouldn't fire. Or there were three of them and they came from different directions. It was hard to swallow.

"You know whose initials they are?"

"AK?"

"Yeah, douche bag, AK. You was talking about him to some people just a couple hours ago."

"Yes." His throat seemed closed. It was hard to squeeze the words out. "Yes, I know whose initials they are."

"Good. Tomorrow you go in and tell those people you were mistaken, douche bag, and that you never seen AK do anything. Right?"

"If I do that you won't bother us?"

"Smart. Smart, douche bag. If you do that you won't never see us again. If you don't we'll come back and kill you both. You see how easy we done up your old lady. We can do you both just as easy. You believe that?"

"Yes."

"Good. And don't think we won't know. You see how fast we knew what was happening? You see how fast we got there. You believe we can find out whatever you do?"

"Yes."

"You gonna do what we told you to do?"

"Yes."

"Good. Your old lady's got a nice-looking pussy. Be a shame to feed it to the worms."

"I . . ." There was a click. The flat voice was gone. Newman put the receiver down very carefully.

Janet said, "Was it them?"

Newman nodded.

Janet said, "Call the cops."

Newman shook his head.

"No?" Janet said. "Why the hell not? If you won't, I will."

He shook his head again. "We can't," he said. "Listen."

Then he told her about the man with the slicked-back hair and the black woman and Corporal Croft and Lieutenant Vincent. He told her about the picture of Adolph Karl in the book and about seeing Adolph Karl in the lineup. He told her about Croft's warning and promise of protection.

"But they knew so fast. They must have a cop on the payroll," Newman said.

She nodded. "What a fucking mess," she said.

"What could I do. I couldn't just keep jogging when the guy shot the girl."

"I know," she said. "I know."

"I mean, I had to do what I thought was right."

"Yes, always. Sometimes, Aaron, I think you read your own books too much." She shook her head angrily. "Never mind. We can't have a damned argument. We have to think what to do."

"We know what to do. I go in tomorrow and tell the cops that I was wrong. And no matter what they say I stick to it and we keep our mouths shut and lie low. Maybe we should go away."

"I can't go away," she said. "I have to work. I have a graduate seminar. I'm up for associate this year. I can't just up and leave, for crissake."

"What's more important," he said, "your life or your fucking job?"

"I can't leave my job," she said. "You go and tell the police you were wrong. And that will be the end of it."

"And it won't bother you to think about it?" he said. "You won't feel like they've demeaned us?" He was sitting on the edge of the bed beside her. He looked at the floor.

She snapped her head around at him. "Demeaned? Who demeaned you? Were you stripped naked and gagged with your own underwear? And tied up so tight you couldn't wiggle your toes? You know anything about that?"

"Did they . . . ?"

"Did they fuck me? Did they feel me up? Isn't that a swell question. No. They just stared at me and didn't say anything and I was lying there on my back with all that rope around me stark naked and they stared at me. You like the scene?"

"Shut up," he said.

"And one of them takes out his knife and puts it down there and I thought he was going to cut me wide open and he cut me on the belly. And I couldn't do a damn thing or even scream. Feel demeaned?"

"Shut up," he said. The trapezius muscles on each side of his neck were bunched and his hands were clenched and clamped between his thighs and the muscles in his forearms bulged.

"And then they left," she said. She was breathing a little hard. Her face was flushed. "And I lay there in the dark all tied up with my underwear stuffed in my mouth and didn't know what to do and couldn't do anything anyway and didn't know if you'd be home or not and couldn't get loose. And you're talking demeaned to me? Who the fuck demeaned you?"

"Shut up," he said. His voice rose and his shoulders shook. "You're demeaned I'm demeaned. You think it's better to sit here and listen to you talk about how some goddamned hoodlums mistreated you and me not around?"

"It's a lot easier than to have it happen to you, buster."

He stood. His back was to her. He looked out the window at the darkened lawn.

"I don't know," he said. "I don't know if it is any easier. What I do know is you're making it harder. You like grinding it into me."

"Maybe. And maybe you liked looking at me when you came in, bound and gagged and naked. Maybe you liked that," she said. "Maybe it turned you on."

Newman half turned away from the window and hit the bedroom door with his right fist. The door didn't break but his hand hurt badly.

4

Lieutenant Vincent stood with his hips resting against his desk and his arms folded across his chest. Croft sat on one straight chair and Newman on the other.

Croft shrugged. "So that's it, Lieutenant. He says he can't make the ID in court. Says he was mistaken."

"Has anyone threatened you, Mr. Newman?"

Newman shook his head.

"No one has said or done anything to change your mind?"

Newman shook his head again. Vincent looked at Croft. They were silent.

Newman said, "I'm sorry, but . . ."

Without looking at him Vincent said, "Shut up."

Croft said to Vincent, "Who knew?"

Vincent said, "You tell me, Bobby. Who knew we had a witness and what his name was?"

"You, me, people in the squadroom. People in Smithfield. Valences from Essex County DA's office." He spread his hands. "Too many, Murray. Got no way to know who they talked to."

"We better try, Bobby. They knew before Newman left this fucking office. You hear what I'm saying?"

Croft nodded.

Newman said, "Wait a minute. Nobody . . ."

Vincent turned toward him. He unfolded his arms and placed his hands palm down on the edge of the desk behind him. "You close it up, scum bag. I got no use for you. You tucked your fucking tail between your fucking legs and hauled ass at the first sign of trouble."

"The hell I . . ."

"Shut up." Vincent straightened from his desk and shoved his face toward Newman, bending forward slightly. "I know somebody threatened you, and I know you're not going to say shit because you think if you're quiet it'll all go away. Maybe it will and maybe Dolph Karl will blast somebody else and it won't be you and you'll shake your head and say 'My my ain't that awful. Why don't those stupid cops do something about it?' Or maybe Dolph will worry about you and maybe he'll send somebody around to make double sure you stay scared and stay quiet."

Newman was silent. The fear twitched and tickled in his stomach.

"You can end it here and now, you got the guts. Or you can be scared and jump at shadows the rest of your life. Or maybe you and your wife and who knows who else can be dead."

Newman could hear that flat uneducated Boston voice on the phone. He shook his head again. "I made an honest mistake, Lieutenant," he said. "I simply made an honest mistake."

Vincent said, "Bobby, get him the fuck away from me." He turned his back and stood looking down at the picture of his family on his desk.

Croft jerked his head and he and Newman got up and left.

"Lieutenant's pissed," Croft said in the hall.

"Corporal Croft, I tell you it was simply a mistake. He wouldn't want me to put an innocent man in jail, would he?"

"Aw, don't bullshit me, Mr. Newman. I know you were threatened or bribed. Lieutenant knows it. You know it. So, I don't know, maybe I don't blame you. Maybe they leaned hard. Maybe they got your wife or kids, it happens. But don't bullshit me."

"Vincent got family?" Newman said.

"Sure," Croft said. "Wife, five kids, I think."

"I suppose he wouldn't back off if they were threatened."

"Vincent? Hell no. He wouldn't back off for anything."

"So what would he do, risk their lives?"

Croft smiled a little. "No, you haven't seen Murray work. I have. He wouldn't back off, and if somebody threatened his family he'd blow him away."

"If he could," Newman said.

Croft was still smiling. "He could," Croft said. "I've seen him work."

They walked down the corridor toward the parking lot.

"The thing is," Croft said, "Murray's probably right. You're making a mistake. You let them do this and they'll be around for the rest of your life. It won't be done like you think it will be. Remember, I told you before. Dolph Karl is a fucking psychopath. We had him on the hook and you let him off. There's no way to know what he'll do."

At the door they stopped. "You change your mind," Croft said, "you give me a call. You have my card."

Newman nodded. "Vincent would kill them?"

Croft nodded. "No doubt in my mind."

"And you?"

Croft was silent for a minute, his hands in his hip pockets. "I guess I'd have to be in the situation. Then I'd see. I don't see too much point to figuring ahead."

Newman started to shake hands, hesitated, and Croft said, "Hell, I'll shake hands with you." He put out his hand and Newman shook it. Then Newman went out into the bright parking lot.

After the air-conditioned building the heat was tangible and startling. His bright blue Jeep was parked against the far wall. As he walked across the half-empty lot he felt obvious and isolated. As if a high camera shot were focused on him. He'd taken the top off the Jeep for the summer, and with the big wheels and the high clearance he felt exposed still as he pulled out onto Commonwealth Avenue.

Jesus Christ I'm scared, he thought as he drove along Commonwealth. He wished he had a gun. He wished Croft were with him. Maybe he could tell the Smithfield police he'd had anonymous threatening phone calls. Maybe they'd put a cruiser nearby. *But if they're watching and they see the cops they'll get us.*

He drove past Boston University into Kenmore Square. One foot was cocked up on the door frame. He wore a blue Levi's shirt, washed often. The sleeves were rolled, the top three buttons were open. As he moved the steering wheel the muscles in his arms swelled beneath his tan.

"Machismo," he said aloud. Jiving it in self-mockery. He looked in the rear-view mirror at the thick brown column of his neck, the strong jaw, the square tanned face. In circles where there weren't any, he was thought a tough guy.

Past Kenmore Square he pulled onto Park Drive and drove through the Fenway. Automatically he looked, as he always did, at the light towers of Fenway Park as they showed above the apartment buildings. They had loomed for him, when he was a boy, like the towers of Camelot.

He went past the Museum of Fine Arts and pulled into the faculty parking lot at Northeastern University. His wife's parking sticker entitled him. Northeastern was an urban university of unrelieved ugliness. Janet's office was in a converted industrial building. Inside, the brick walls and hardwood floors had been veneered with paint and vinyl and the open spaces partitioned with wallboard. It was air-conditioned. In Janet's office there were another woman and two men. Newman knew them. He didn't like them much. He was jealous of Janet's work and her friends at work and her commitment to both the work and the friends.

As he came to her door she was talking animatedly. Her eyes were bright and wide, her hands moved. Her color was high. *Goddamn isn't she something*. There was a faint red line on her left wrist, where last night the rope had marked it. He felt anxiety heavy in his stomach, but also faintly, around the edges, desire as he remembered her naked helplessness.

He stepped around the corner of her office door and said, "Newman's the name, words are my game."

Janet stopped talking and smiled at him and waved.

"Margie," he said, "how are you? Jim? Charles?"

They spoke to him. He made them a little uneasy, he knew. He had been reviewed in *Time* and *Newsweek* and been on the *Today* show. For them he was a celebrity. And a celebrity in the field where they would care. They were all English professors, he was a writer. Always inside them was the war; Newman understood it. Always there was the disdain for his popularity and envy of his success. He liked making them uncomfortable.

Janet said, "What are you doing here? Did you have your appointment?"

"Yeah," Newman said. "I had it. It went okay. They were a little upset, but nothing they could do."

Margie was small and very slim with perfectly black hair and good features. She was much younger than Janet. "Anything wrong?" she said.

"No," Janet said. "Just some business that had to be done. It involved returning some merchandise and I was afraid it could be unpleasant." She smiled. "That's why I had Aaron do it."

"Man's work," he said. They were very liberated here in the English department. He loved to scandalize them. If only mildly. "How about you and me, little lady, we go down to Chris's Place and have a few drinks and dinner."

"Aaron, I have my car," she said.

"So drive down, meet me there. Or drive down in the Jeep with me and we'll come back and get your car."

"I'm not riding in the Jeep and having my hair blow all over the place."

He took a big breath. "Okay, then, ride down in your car and meet me."

"Okay, but I'll be late. There's a curriculum committee meeting and it's important. I won't be able to get there for another hour."

"Course, don't want to miss that curriculum committee meeting. Probably couldn't have it without you. What are you going to do at this meeting, plan the next meeting?"

"Aaron, don't be a pain in the ass. You go down and have a few beers with Chris and I'll come down after our meeting."

"Yeah, okay, when can I expect you? You know how you are." He looked at the two men. One was tall and willowy with a full beard and small round gold-rimmed glasses. The other was middle-sized and trim with a European-cut three-piece suit and a Phi Beta Kappa key on his watch chain. *Half his salary on the goddamned suit.*

"I'll be there in an hour, I already said that. The meeting will have to end at six because people have classes at six-thirty. Go ahead. I'll be there."

He nodded, smiled at the four of them, and turned to go. He paused next to the medium man in the three-piece suit. "Charles," he said. "You are a regular fashion plate."

He was close to Charles and was aware of how much bigger he was than Charles. He wanted Charles to feel that, to let the sense of his mass sink in. Charles smiled vaguely.

"I wish I could dress as you do, Aaron, and stay home all day and cash big checks, but some of us aren't so lucky, or talented, maybe."

Newman grinned. "That's true," he said. He waved his hand at all of them again and went out. *Jesus Christ, we got the biggest problem of our fucking life and she's got a curriculum meeting. Nice how she'd give up anything to be with me. Nice how she's always there when I'm feeling bad. Very fucking nice.* He got in his Jeep and drove toward the waterfront. His eyes stung as if he would cry. But there were no tears.

5

At forty-seven Chris Hood stood six feet tall and weighed 190. He had a black belt in karate, could bench-press 375 pounds. The skin on his body was too tight to pinch. In 1950 he had jumped into Wonson, Korea, with the Second Ranger battalion, been captured, escaped, returned to his unit, and won the Distinguished Service Cross. From 1956 to 1959 he returned punts and kickoffs for the Detroit Lions. He had been cut six weeks before he qualified for a pension. He came back to Boston and worked as a bartender and a bouncer in several different clubs and finally in 1976 opened a heavily mortgaged pub/restaurant in the area of Quincy Market. He sat at the bar with Newman and sipped Perrier water with a twist of lime while Newman drank Beck's beer.

"Janet coming down?" he said.

Newman said, "Yes. She's got a meeting first."

The room was dim and air-conditioned. The bar itself was mahogany. Behind the bar on the wall above the display of bottles was the mounted head of a grizzly bear Hood had shot in Alaska.

"Hear anything from Kathy?" Newman said.

Hood laughed. "Every time I'm a day late with the alimony."

"How're the kids?"

"Okay, I guess." Hood looked at the grizzly head on the wall. "I don't see much of them, to tell you the truth. You hear from Karen?"

"Yeah," Newman said. "She's in Amsterdam. And next week she's going to Paris."

"When's she get back?"

"September, just before school starts."

"How about Sandy?"

"She's in Cleveland, she's dancing in a road company revival of *Carousel*. They're supposed to be in Boston in November and she says she'll be able to come home a couple of days."

Hood looked at Newman's glass, saw it was empty, and nodded at the bartender. He brought a new bottle.

"Your kids are doing good," Hood said. "They're going where they want to. They're learning what they like. They're not hung up on *supposed to* and all that shit. You and Janet have done a good job. Hope Kathy doesn't fuck mine up."

Hood had a dark, thick moustache. His hair was curly and short with no gray in it. He wore blue-tinted aviator glasses.

Newman drank half his beer at a swallow. "You killed people in Korea, right?"

Hood nodded. "Sure," he said. "We were supposed to. Didn't you?"

Newman shook his head. "No. I don't think so. There were some skirmishes and stuff, but I don't think I ever shot anyone."

"Just like hunting," Hood said. "Nothing personal. You get in a fire fight and it's kind of fun. It's exciting. Unless you get killed."

Newman drank the rest of his beer. The bartender brought another.

"Ever kill anyone except in Korea?"

Hood raised his eyebrows. "Nice question," he said. "If I had would I admit it?"

Newman said, "No, I guess you wouldn't. Do you think you could?"

"Kill someone, sure. If I had a reason. You got someone in mind? I get through here at three."

Two women came into the bar. One wore white pants and a blue-striped halter top that showed a lot of cleavage. The other had on a denim jumpsuit with rhinestone trim and a pair of sling-strap high heels. The cuffs of her pants were rolled up in a six-inch-wide turn. They sat in a booth behind Newman and Hood and looked for a long time at Hood.

"They're both looking at you, Chris," Newman said. "Must have seen my wedding ring."

Hood turned and looked steadily at both women for perhaps a minute. Both of them reddened. One said, "What are you looking at?"

Hood said, "I'm not sure," politely and turned back toward the bar.

The bartender brought Newman another beer and looked at Hood's glass of half-drunk Perrier. Hood shook his head slightly and the bartender went away.

"Three billion people in the world," Newman said, "and I end up living next to a guy who looks like Robert Redford."

"He's blond," Hood said.

"Oh yeah."

"You look like you've lost a little weight," Hood said.

"Oh yeah, maybe a few pounds. I'm fighting it all the time. You know what happened to me last night?"

"You got laid?"

"No." Then he told Hood everything that had happened. He spoke softly, leaning toward Hood so that no one would hear him. And he spoke rapidly but with very little inflection. Hood listened and said nothing.

"I'm out taking a pleasant little run for my weight and my health, you know. And now gangsters are threatening me and tying up my wife and I don't know what the fuck to do. I mean, *Runner's World* doesn't cover this kind of thing."

"So that's why you were asking me about killing people."

Janet Newman came in the front door wearing huge sunglasses with wire rims, and walked the length of the bar, slowly, as her eyes adjusted to the light. She had on a white gauze dress and black high heels and carried a black shoulder bag. Three men at the bar turned to watch her walk past. When she reached them she kissed Hood on the cheek and slid in beside Newman.

"Not bad for an old broad," Hood said.

"Want something?" Newman said.

"Perrier with a twist of whatever," Janet said. Hood motioned to the bartender.

No vices, Newman thought. *Won't get drunk, won't get fat, won't get out of control. Some fun, a glass of soda water.* "Better be careful on the Perrier," Newman said. "You know how you get after three. Just climb all over me."

She smiled. "Dream on, Aaron," she said. "Have a rich fantasy life."

Hood was looking at her. "You okay?"

"Sure," Janet said. "Why shouldn't I be okay?"

"Aaron told me about last night," Hood said.

Janet frowned. She looked at Aaron. "Was that smart?"

Newman shrugged. "I thought Chris could help me make sense out of it. Why not tell him?" Newman drank beer.

"It's not Chris," Janet said. "But I don't think it's wise to talk about it to anyone. If it stops here that's one thing, but who else will you tell? Have a few beers and . . . " She spread her hands, palms up.

Hood said, "We were quiet about it. I won't say a word. Who the hell else do I talk to but you?"

"And just what was Chris going to help you make sense out of," Janet said.

"The whole thing. The shooting, the way they treated you, the way I had to go and tell the cops I was mistaken. The lieutenant called me yellow." Newman drank more beer. "But I can't let them harm you. Christ, you're my whole life."

Janet said, "They threatened to harm you too."

Newman shrugged and looked at the bar top and shook his head as if to clear it.

"Or the girls," he said. "You know what I'm like. I'm a husband and a father before I'm anything else. It's what makes life purposeful."

"How about the books," Hood said.

"They help, but they're not family. That's what I do, not what I am."

"You write good books, Aaron," Hood said.

"Yeah, about courage and the matter of honor and how things heal stronger at the break."

"Best since Hemingway," Hood said. Janet sipped her Perrier.

"And then two bums come around and humiliate my wife and I roll over and make gestures of submission."

"Oh, Aaron, don't be so goddamned melodramatic," Janet said. "What else are you expected to do?"

The bartender brought more beer. Newman finished his glass and poured more.

"I could kill them," he said.

Something stirred in the back of Chris Hood's eyes and tugged briefly at the corners of his mouth.

Janet said, "Oh, Aaron, grow up. You don't even know who they are."

Newman still stared at the bar top, his head lowered between his shoulders. "I know who he is," he said.

"Aaron," Janet said, "you know how you are when you're drinking."

"I'm not drunk," Newman said.

"That's one of the things you always say when you're drinking."

"You think I'd be scared to?"

"Kill someone?"

"Yeah."

"Aaron, it is a little unusual to sit about in a restaurant and discuss killing someone."

"You think I'd be scared?"

"I don't know. Would you?"

"You wouldn't, would you?"

"Be scared to kill someone?"

"Yeah."

"No."

"You feel like killing anyone when they were tying you up and maybe copping a little feel while they were doing it?"

Janet shivered. Hood looked at her and then at Newman. The muscles at his jaw-hinge moved slightly.

"You feel like killing anybody then?" Newman said.

"Yes." Janet's voice was very soft and it hissed out between her teeth.

"So why don't we?"

Janet looked at Hood.

"He's serious, Janet," Hood said.

She poked at the slice of lime in her glass of Perrier water. "And you?"

Hood said, "Whenever you need help, I'll help you. Whatever it is. You know that."

"You're willing to kill someone?"

Hood shrugged. "Whatever," he said.

"I'd do it for him," Newman said. He finished his beer. "They did cop a little feel, didn't they?" There was sweat on his forehead. He felt that odd mixture of lust and horror he'd felt before when he'd found her on the bed.

Janet looked at him without speaking. She ran the ball of her index finger around the rim of her glass.

"Didn't they?"

She shook her head.

"Like hell," Newman said. "They touched you. Didn't they?" He felt desperation. He had to know.

Hood said, "Aaron, for crissake."

Newman said, "Didn't they?"

Very softly Janet said, "No. They made me touch them."

Newman slammed his open palm on the bar top. Hood said, as softly as Janet had spoken, "Jesus."

Newman said, "How . . ." and stopped. Hood looked at him once and shook his head.

Janet said, very softly and with no apparent emotion, "Yes. I want to kill them. This morning when I woke up I was afraid and didn't remember why. You know that feeling. You wake up and you think *Oh something is awful but I forgot what* and then you remember, and I remember how they made me touch them. And I remember how helpless I was first when they made me touch them and then when they tied me up and I couldn't move and they gagged me and I couldn't talk or even spit. I remember that feeling of nakedness and helplessness and every morning when I wake up I will be afraid. And all the time I walk around with that feeling in my stomach of sinkingness and afraid. All the time I think *What if they come back* and I feel helpless. It's not a good feeling for me. I need to control things. I need to feel that I am in control. You know that, Aaron. I've always needed to manage things, otherwise they frighten me. They get out of control. I can't function like this. I say 'I'll not let it happen.' I say 'I'll put it aside and go on and do my business and my work and not think about it,' but it's always there and every morning I'll wake up frightened."

Hood put his hand lightly on her forearm. Newman was silent. Both men were leaning forward toward her to listen as she spoke very softly.

"I've got to get back in control," she said. "It will

destroy me and destroy us. I can't be anything you'd want to live with unless I have control."

"We'll get it back," Newman said. He spoke very carefully so as not to slur his words.

"I want to shoot him," Janet said. "I want to shoot him and the two men who came and tied me up. I want them to die. I want to be free of this."

"Could it be done, Chris?" Newman said.

"Sure. Sure it could."

"Would you do it with me?"

"Sure," Hood said. "Sure I would."

6

They had moved to a booth and a waitress had brought them a platter of sandwiches.

"If we shot him," Hood said, "it would solve a lot of problems. You'd bring him, in a sense, to justice."

Newman had been drinking beer for two hours and it had begun to show in his speech. "And we'd see to it that he hurt no one else." He had trouble separating the *to* and the *it*. "That would make me feel better. It bothers me, he walks around loose."

"And we'd be out from under," Janet said. "The son of a bitch."

"Is it just revenge?" Newman said. He ate a triangular sandwich and gestured with his empty beer bottle toward the waitress. She brought him another.

Janet said, "I want revenge and I want to be sure that what happened to me never happens again. I don't mind killing somebody. I don't give a damn about that."

"Course you never have," Hood said softly.

"Killed somebody? No. But the thought doesn't bother me."

Newman said, "For crissake, Janet, keep it down."

She cocked her head at him and the flint edge came into her voice. It always scared him when the edge came. "Oh, you find me loud? Am I embarrassing you?"

"No, it's just that if we do it, we wouldn't want people to say they heard us talking about it." He felt as if he'd been bad. His stomach ached slightly with apprehension. *Her disapproval is devastating. She just looks hard at me and I get scared. Talk about pussy-whipped.* "We are talking about murder."

Hood said, "He's right, Janet."

She smiled at Hood and nodded. "I know, Chris, it's one of the problems of the whole problem, isn't it? We have to kill this man Karl so that neither the police nor the gangsters know we did it, or even suspect us. I assume his friends or whatever would want to revenge him even if they only suspected."

"And they're not concerned with rules of evidence, Janet," Hood said.

"So we can't even be spotted," Janet said. "If they recognize us, we're dead."

Hood smiled. "That sounds about right," he said.

"We're still talking about murder here," Newman said.

Hood sipped at his Perrier water. Even in the booth with the Newmans he seemed remote, partly in the shadow. They each leaned forward, arms on the table. He leaned back in the corner of the booth.

"What difference does it make what you call it," Janet Newman said. "Don't play word games. We have a problem here and we're thinking about a solution. You had the original idea."

Newman looked at his beer glass. "This isn't a goddamned curriculum question. We're talking about a human life."

Janet made a hissing sound. "I know what we're talking about," she said. "I had a lot of chance to think about it last night while I was lying on the bed tied up. It's not going to happen to me again. That's a goal. I'm looking for a process by which we can achieve that goal."

"Process-oriented," Newman said. "Really sharpened the old management skills being chairman of that curriculum committee. 'Scuse me, chairperson."

Janet Newman said, "Oh, Jesus Christ, Aaron."

Chris Hood said, "Excuse me a moment." He slid out of the booth and walked halfway down the bar. A heavy man in a white three-piece suit and a black shirt with no tie was leaning over the left shoulder of a woman at the bar. She was wearing an ankle-length flowered dress and sandals. As Hood approached, the woman said something to the man and shook her head hard.

Hood put his left hand gently on the man's shoulder and smiled and murmured something.

The man said, "Who the fuck are you?"

Hood murmured again to the woman. She nodded.

The man said, "Get your hands off my shoulder, Jack, or there's gonna be trouble."

Hood's hand tightened slightly on the man's shoulder, and he murmured again and nodded toward the door.

The man said, "Fuck you, buddy," and Hood hit him in the kidneys with his right fist. The punch traveled six inches. The man yelped. Hood's left hand slid down the man's arm, got the wrist, and levered it up behind the man's back. His right hand took hold of the man's collar, and Hood and the man in the white suit walked very fast toward the front door and outside.

The bartender put another drink in front of the woman in the long flowered dress, and Hood came back in the bar, walked down to the Newmans' booth, and sat down. He sipped at his Perrier.

"Sorry," he said.

"I was about to rush out and join you," Newman said. "What happened out there?"

Hood smiled and shook his head. "Nothing," he said. "Man just decided to move to another bar."

"What if the man is too hard to handle?" Janet said.

"They usually aren't," Hood said. "And besides"—he took a two dollar roll of nickels out of his coat pocket—"I have a helper."

Newman laughed. "All right, Chris," he said. "Want me to work here on busy nights? We could really do a tune on some guy."

"How about Adolph Karl," Janet said. "Can you do a tune on him?"

Newman finished his beer and belched. "I bet we could," he said. "Chris and I? Huh? What you say, Chris. Can we take him?"

"What's that the man said once," Hood answered. "To kill a man you need three things: the gun and the balls?"

"We can get the gun okay," Newman said. He ran *get* and *the* together. "And we got the rest." Newman's color was high and he drummed on the table edge with both hands.

Janet Newman said, "I'll be interested to see how you feel about it tomorrow."

"Why," Newman said, "cause I been drinking? I'm not drunk."

"Why not sleep on it. And you might want to think what you're trying to involve Chris in."

"For crissake, don't you want me to do it? A minute ago you were talking like you wanted me to do it. You want me to do it, I'll do it."

The waitress appeared, looked at Newman's empty glass. Hood shook his head very slightly and the waitress went away.

"Because I want you to?" Janet said.

"Yeah. You want it. I'll get it for you."

"Not because you want it?"

"It don't matter what I want. I do whatever you want, babe. You want something done, I'm your man."

"So it's all up to me," Janet said.

"Some of it is up to me, Janet," Hood said. He was sitting back in his corner, and the shadow of the booth hid his eyes. "It's up to me how far I get involved in this."

"Of course, Chris. If you don't involve yourself, I very much doubt if Aaron will. Even if he thinks so now."

"Bullshit," Newman said. "I'll do it with him or without. I got you, babe, I don't need anything else."

Hood smiled and was silent.

"Always self-sacrifice, always the martyr to love," Janet Newman said. "If you do this it will be because you want to. I'm not going to be the one."

"Fuck this," Newman said and stood up. "I'm going home. You coming?"

"I have my car," Janet said, "remember?"

Newman said, "Yes, so you do," and turned and walked out of the bar.

In the booth Janet and Hood were silent. Then Janet said, "Chris. He's going to do it, the son of a bitch. Or I'll do it myself. Those bastards. They will not do that to me again."

"You're thinking about revenge, Janet, and safety."

"So what."

"He's thinking about honor and courage, maybe justice."

"Shit."

"Not to him it isn't. They're hard things to think about. Being the kind of man he thinks he ought to be is hard. It's a burden."

"Being the kind of woman he thinks I ought to be isn't very easy either," she said. "I just think that killing Adolph Karl is the only intelligent solution to the problem we've got. It will serve as justice for the young woman he killed, it will prevent him from doing it again, it will take our own lives out of jeopardy, it will, I admit this, ease my own sense of violation. And it will solve Aaron's problems of honor and manhood or whatever you think is bothering him."

"What do you think is bothering him?"

"Oh God, Chris, I don't know and I'm sick of trying to figure it out. He's not a man, he's a big child. Everything has to be romance and chivalry and . . ." She gestured aimlessly with her hand.

"And a code of behavior," Hood said. "I read the books. That's not always a bad thing, Janet."

"Live with it awhile," she said.

Hood was silent.

"Would it bother you to do it, Chris? To kill Adolph Karl?"

"No."

"Why not?"

"I agree with your summary of the situation. It seems your best move."

"It'll bother Aaron, I can assure you."

"He's never done it before," Hood said.

"Kill someone?"

"Yes."

"Neither have I," Janet said, "but it doesn't bother me."

"I've got another edge on Aaron," Hood said.

"You're probably in better shape," Janet said.

"No," Hood said. "I kind of like it."

7

Newman woke in the morning uneasy and feeling guilt. As always after he'd been drinking he ran back in his mind to see if he'd done anything bad. He felt hot with embarrassment that he'd tried to swagger with Chris about being a bouncer in his pub.

The air conditioner was humming, Janet was still asleep, her back to him, her hair up, a blue scarf tied around it. There was an old maple tree in the front yard. Its trunk was four feet in diameter. The thick healthy green leaves moved gently against the sky outside the bedroom window. He felt the stab of fear as he thought of Adolph Karl. Two cops had called him a psychopath. He'd talked with such conviction last night about killing him.

He slid under the covers over against Janet. His pelvis pressed against her buttocks. He put his left arm over her and put his hand on her breast. She was wearing a bra. *Like armor,* he thought. *Always a bra, underpants, pj's, socks, no matter how hot it is. Must be security or something. Sometimes a fucking bathrobe.* She rolled over onto her stomach away from his hand.

"I gather," he said, "you don't care for a little nooky?"

"Un-unh," she murmured, still half-asleep.

He rolled back over to his own side of the bed and lay on his back. His throat felt tight and again his eyes stung but no tears came. He thought of her as he had seen her on the bed the night before. Naked and helpless. *Couldn't even spit.* Desire buzzed in his stomach. He looked at her beside him. She was on her stomach, her face turned away. Except for the slight rise and fall of her back as she breathed she was inert. One of her hair rollers had come loose and was half hanging out from her blue scarf.

"You want me to kill some guy for you," he said.

She moved slightly, still asleep, and said, "Ummm."

He laughed without humor, or sound, and got up. He slept naked. In the bathroom mirror he looked at himself. He had the weight lifter's mass. Pectoral muscles, deltoids, triceps, all over-developed. But there was fat, too, a roll around his waist that thickened his whole body, flesh that softened and sagged his chest over the big pectoral muscles. His upper eyelids had sagged so that the top round of his eye was covered, and the flesh under his chin was loose so that if he tucked his chin back at all his neck disappeared.

He flexed at the mirror. He looked better when he flexed. What seemed soft was suddenly revealed as hard, what might have been fat was in fact shown to be muscle. *Not bad for forty-six. If I could only drop twenty pounds I'd be splendid for forty-six.*

In the shower he thought about Adolph Karl. *But would it be right,* he thought. *Do I have the right to take the law into my own hands. Christ, I sound like a comic strip. Who was that masked man anyway? But*

*do I? But if I don't, how can I stand being dishonored
so?* "I could not love thee half so much loved I not
honor more." *I wonder if Richard Lovelace was married.* Was he just worrying about the ethics of it to
avoid doing it? Was he simply scared?

He lathered his hair with apple-scented shampoo
and let the hot water run over him rinsing the shampoo away. *Let's look at the problem of scared.* He
tried to examine himself, to study his spiritual condition the way one might examine a painting. But his
spiritual condition was evasive. It wouldn't stay in
frame, it shifted. *Like looking at an electron,* he
thought. *The act of observation changes its behavior.
Yes, I'm scared, but is that why I'm hesitating on this
thing? Chris wouldn't hesitate. Chris would go right
to it. Ah, but I'm not Chris, nor was meant to be.*

He shut off the water and stepped out of the
shower. *The world is out of joint.* He toweled dry and
went back upstairs to the bedroom to dress. He never
used the upstairs bathroom. She used it to get dressed
for work. A steamy shower would ruin her hair.

The bedroom was empty. She was in the bathroom
getting ready for work. He dressed and made the bed,
tightening the sheets, making careful hospital corners,
smoothing the quilt over the pillows. She never made
the bed right, she simply rolled the quilt up over
sheets and pillows so there was a sense of lumpiness
under the quilt, and when you got in at night the
sheets were wrinkly.

He had breakfast on the table when she came into
the kitchen. As he heard her step on the back stairs he
poured the coffee, and everything was ready when
she sat down. There were melon slices arranged on a
plate, and toasted oatmeal bread, and strawberry jam,

and coffee. Almost never did either of them eat the melon, but he liked the look of it on the table.

She'd spent more than an hour making up and getting her hair organized. She wore a white muslin shirt with loose sleeves and a slotted neck, and high-waisted apricot-colored pants with a draw waist and tapered legs over high heels. She smelled of perfume.

"Christ," he said, "aren't you beautiful."

She said, "Thank you."

"You come to any conclusion about what we were saying last night?"

She looked at him over a triangle of toast. "Have you?"

"No."

"Why don't you talk with Chris?"

"How can he help?"

"He's decisive," she said, "and he seems to have some understanding of some male hang-up you may have, which I don't seem to."

"Like honor?"

She gestured with her toast and shrugged.

"Talk to him."

"You want it done, don't you? You want it done and you figure Chris will talk me into it."

"Whatever he did, Chris would do it and have it done," she said.

"Like that drunk last night, a couple of quiet words, the guy doesn't respond and *vap* in the kidneys and out the door. You like that?"

"I don't like uncertainty. I don't like having someone walking around who might, anytime, decide to degrade me or kill me. And I have no say in the matter."

"I won't let him touch you again."

"So how will you stop it. Follow me everywhere with a gun? Hire bodyguards? There's only one way to control this situation."

"So why don't you do it? You're the big fucking feminist. You want Karl shot why don't you shoot him?"

"While you're doing what? Lifting weights and looking at yourself in the mirror? Home baking a cake? I've never fired a gun in my life. I'm tough but I'm not physically strong. You're big and strong. Aren't you?"

He felt trapped and confused. He swayed his head back and forth, staring at the tabletop. "Why don't you leave me the fuck alone," he said. His voice was thick and shaky.

"Why do you persist in seeing this as something I'm doing to you," she said. "Why do you want to see yourself attacked."

"Don't give me that encounter-group bullshit. Use your assertiveness jargon someplace else. I don't want to see myself attacked. You are pushing and pushing. You want something done you don't let up. You keep on and keep on. I'm not talking about it anymore. Now that's it. You insensitive son of a bitch."

The lines at the corners of her eyes deepened and her perfectly made-up face darkened slightly. She looked at the kitchen clock.

"Jesus Christ," she said, "I'm late. Aaron, you've got to deal with this. We've got to be able to talk about it. I was involved in this problem myself. Remember?"

He brought his open hand down hard on the tabletop. Coffee spilled. "I said I wouldn't talk about it. You want to keep grinding it into me? You want to keep reminding me what some guy did to my wife and I haven't lifted a finger?" He raised his hand again, clenched it into a fist, and brought it back down on the table, twisting his shoulder and neck as if he were trying to hammer a hole through the table-top.

"I gotta go," Janet said. "I'm late. I gotta go. But I won't give up. We've got to talk about this."

Newman hit the table again. His wife picked up her briefcase and her book bag, tan with a green design, and her purse and went out the kitchen door to her car.

Newman sat at the kitchen table and stared at the *Today* show. He was breathing hard as if he'd run a distance. His sight blurred with tears. With his clenched fist he hit the table softly. Barely moving his fist, over and over.

He was still sitting at the table at nine-thirty when Chris Hood walked across the backyard from his small white house to Newman's big one. He came in the kitchen door without knocking.

"Coffee?" he said.

Newman said, "Instant," and nodded at the jar on the counter. "Water's probably still pretty hot."

Hood turned the gas flame on under the kettle, got a cup from the cabinet, and put a spoonful of instant coffee in it. He got two slices of oatmeal bread out of the second drawer to the right of the sink and put them in the toaster. When steam came from the kettle he made coffee, put margarine on his toast, and sat down at the table. He had on a blue T-shirt that said Adidas in white lettering across the front and he looked, as he moved and the small muscles played intricately beneath the skin, like a fine mechanism in perfect working order.

"You want to talk?" Hood said.

"About what?" Newman said.

"About us killing this guy, Karl," Hood said. "You got any jam?"

"Refrigerator," Newman said. Hood went to the refrigerator and took out a two-pound jar of strawberry preserves.

"Good," Hood said. "Smucker's, they're the best kind."

Newman nodded. "You and me?" he said.

"Yes." Hood put strawberry jam on his toast.

"You and me go out and actually shoot this guy Karl?"

"Yes."

"Why?"

"Janet's right," Hood said. "Everything she said. It's the only way to go."

"Maybe," Newman said. "But why you?"

Hood grinned. "What are friends for?"

Newman shook his head. There was no humor in his voice. "Why?" he said.

"It's true," Hood said. "I'm living alone. Jerry can manage the place for me if he has to. It's the kind of thing I can do."

"Kill someone?"

"Well, scuffle, fight, hit, handle trouble, you know."

Newman continued to look at Hood.

"I'm good with my hands," Hood said.

Newman nodded. "Yeah, I know that, Chris, but"— Newman put his palms up—"kill someone? Someone you don't even know?"

"I know you. And Janet. And it's what I can do."

"This is their business, you know. They're professionals. What if they kill us instead?"

"No point playing tennis with the net down," Hood said. "It's part of the fun."

"The threat of death."

"Sure. No fun if there wasn't some strain to it. Not too much point in doing it."

"I thought you wanted to do it because it was a logical way to solve our problem."

Hood said, "No. I think you should do it for that reason. I'm willing to help for other reasons. And besides, I know you. It'll eat your liver till you've done something."

"Or Janet will," Newman said.

Hood said nothing.

"Okay," Newman said. "Let's do it."

8

Newman looked at the gun rack in Chris Hood's den. There was a lever-action Winchester .30/30, a semi-automatic M1 carbine with a fifteen-round clip, a five-shot 12-gauge Ithaca pump gun, a Ruger .44 magnum bushgun. In a locked case beneath the gun rack was a 9mm Walther P-38 automatic pistol, a hammerless Smith & Wesson .32 revolver with a nickel plating, an Army-issue Colt .45 automatic pistol, a bone-handled bowie knife with a nine-inch blade, and a skinning knife with a four-inch blade that folded into the handle. In a wall cabinet beside the gun rack there was ammunition for all the weapons. The guns were all clean and filmed with a fine glaze of oil. The stocks of the long guns were polished, the holsters of the handguns were soft leather well treated. In the dim quiet room with the air-conditioner humming its soft white sound, the guns seemed precise and orderly and full of promise. Newman felt still and calm looking at them.

"Take the .32," Hood said. "Five shots, small, easy to carry. Wear it on your belt and hang the shirt outside."

Newman took the handgun and aimed it at a knot-hole in the paneled wall. He slid it in and out of the soft leather holster. He slipped his belt through the holster slot and redid the belt. He let the tails of his tattersall shirt hang out over his belt. The gun was invisible. He pulled it and aimed at the knothole again.

Hood took a box of shells from the cabinet and handed them to Newman.

"It breaks here," he said, taking the revolver from Newman and opening it. Newman fed five bright cartridges into the cylinder, closed the gun, and slipped it into his holster under his shirt.

"What about a permit?" Newman said.

Hood said, "I've got one."

Newman said, "But I haven't. All I've got is an FID card. I can't carry this on your permit."

Hood smiled. "We're setting out to commit murder, Aaron. I wouldn't sweat the unlicensed gun too much."

Newman nodded. Hood put on a shoulder holster and slipped the P-38 in it. He put an extra clip of ammunition in his hip pocket and the folding knife in his side pocket. He handed the carbine to Newman.

"Remember how to fire this?"

"Yes," Newman said. "It's one of the things you don't forget. Like bike-riding."

"Or sex," Hood said. He picked up the Winchester and a box of ammunition. "Come on," he said. "Let's get to it."

"I think Karl might catch on," Newman said, "if he saw us walking up his driveway like this."

"We'll stash the long guns in the car. I just figured we'd be better to have them handy."

"And you might want to put on something over the shoulder holster."

"Smart," Hood said. "You writers are a smart breed."

They walked through Hood's small immaculate kitchen. On a peg by the back door was a short-sleeved cotton safari jacket. Hood put it on. They put the carbine and Winchester, wrapped in a blanket, behind the back seat in Hood's red and white 1976 Bronco.

"You got the address?" Hood said.

"473 Lynn Shore Drive. If it's the same Adolph Karl. It was the only one in the phone book."

"Probably him."

"Would he be listed?"

"Why not. Don't thugs make phone calls?"

Newman said, "Yes they do. Sometimes they make house calls."

They drove from Smithfield to Lynn and through Lynn to the road that ran along the ocean. Number 473 was a three-story brick house on the Lynn-Swampscott line. Around it was a strip of dry lawn no more than three feet wide. On either side the neighbors' houses were close. There was a two-car garage and in the cement driveway that connected it to the street was parked a dark blue Lincoln with an orange vinyl top.

"That's the car," Newman said. He felt the tension again in his solar plexus. He put his hand down on the butt of the gun under his shirt. "It must be the right place," he said.

Hood drove on past and turned left at a drugstore a block beyond Karl's house. He parked.

"Karl ever see you?"

Newman shook his head.

"How about the guys that laid it on Janet? They see you?"

Newman shook his head again.

"Then nobody in this group should know what you look like."

"True," Newman said. His voice was hoarse.

"So let's stroll back and look at the building a bit."

They got out. Hood locked the car. They walked back a block along the seawall side of the street. Below them the beach was littered and beyond the beach waves rolled in from the open ocean. Across the harbor the turtle back of Nahant rose at the end of its causeway. Behind them a massive restaurant looked out over a cove where fishing boats rocked at tether.

They leaned against the seawall and looked at Karl's house. On the ocean side there was a sunporch, the windows closed by venetian blinds. Above the sunporch the house rose two more stories. The third story looked cramped beneath the slate mansard roof. The house actually fronted on a small side street. Four windows on the first floor, five on the second, two A-dormers through the slate roof on the third. There were venetian blinds in each of these windows.

"Nice-looking house," Hood said.

"No land, though," Newman said. "Right up against the neighbors."

"Yeah, you could reach out your window and into theirs."

"No place to sneak around and shoot through the windows."

"Even if there were," Hood said, "the damned blinds are closed. You couldn't see what to shoot at."

It was a bright summer day, but not hot. The wind

off the ocean was steady and pleasant. Newman felt strong. He was conscious of the thickness of his arms and chest, the resiliency of his legs, the small, good weight of the gun under his shirt. He realized he wasn't afraid. *On the prowl,* he thought. *That's what makes the difference. I'm not slinking around scared, wondering what he's going to do. I'm after him. He should be scared.* "Running makes you scared," Newman said.

Hood said, "What?"

"It's running makes you scared," Newman said. "Now I'm chasing instead of running, I don't feel scared."

"Yeah," Hood said. He was looking at Karl's house. "There's no damned cover," he said. "No buildings we could get in and shoot from, no place where we could be under cover and wait. We could shoot from the car, but it's difficult driving and hard to get out of here. Traffic's bad. There's a cop up there on the corner. Probably usually is."

"The gun helps, too," Newman said.

"Helps what?" Hood said.

"Not being scared. The gun makes you feel good. Like you can't be overpowered."

"I wouldn't count on can't," Hood said. "The gun makes it harder, but it doesn't make you bulletproof, you know?"

Newman nodded. "What do we do now?" he said.

"I figure we watch," Hood said. "We get a feel for how this guy functions. See if he goes to work or something. Get him outside the house we may have a better chance."

"We could go right up and knock on the door and when someone opened it in we go with the guns." As he said it, Newman hoped Hood would disapprove. Newman didn't like the idea as he said it.

"Some things wrong with that, Aaron. We don't know who or what's in there. Guy like Karl may have some bodyguards. Also if there were other people there besides Karl, like his wife or kids or whatever, we'd probably have to kill them, or they'd be able to identify us to the cops, or Karl's friends or whoever. Besides, a guy like Karl probably doesn't just open the door when someone knocks. Even if we didn't get hurt, if we tried it and didn't get in, we'd make him suspicious. We don't want him suspicious."

"That's for sure," Newman said.

"We'll split it up," Hood said. "I'll be in the car up the road. If Karl comes out and gets in the car, you turn and look out to sea. I'll come down and pick you up."

"Okay. And if no one goes anyplace?"

"Come supper time we go home," Hood said. "What else can we do."

"And come back tomorrow?"

"And come back tomorrow," Hood said. "Unless you get bored and want to quit."

"I won't quit," Newman said. "Besides, as long as I'm watching him I know he's not after me."

Hood nodded and walked up the street to where the car was parked.

9

At seven-twenty in the evening, Newman walked up along the seawall and got into Hood's car, parked on the street in front of the drugstore.

"That's it," he said. "If I stand there another five minutes my toenails will fall off."

Hood started the Bronco and they drove back past Karl's house. It was as impervious and blank as it had been since they arrived.

"Well, the first day wasn't too thrilling," Newman said.

"One day it will be," Hood said. "Things take time. You gotta be careful, and watch, and work out what you're going to do, and know what you're up against. Takes time."

"Umm."

At eight they pulled into Newman's driveway. Janet's maroon MG was there with the top up. "Never mess the hair," Newman said.

Hood smiled. The house seemed quiet. Newman felt the threat of its silence.

"Come on in for a beer," he said to Hood.

"Sure."

They got out of the car and Newman put his hand on the butt of the gun under his shirt. Janet appeared in the doorway. Newman moved his hand away.

"Where've you been," she said. "I was getting worried."

Newman smiled. "I'll tell you, when we get in. Come on, Chris."

They sat at the kitchen table and Newman got two beers from the refrigerator.

"I'll have a little wine, Aaron," Janet said. He poured her a glass of white wine.

"You hungry?" Newman said to Hood.

"For sure," Hood said.

"There's steaks in the freezer. You want one, Jan?"

"Yes, I'd love one. A small one, maybe half."

"Yeah, you got a real fat problem," Newman said. He drank half the beer at one pull on the can.

"Well, what have you guys been doing?" Janet said.

Newman put the three steaks, still frozen, in a fry pan on the stove and turned the gas on medium. He drank the other half of the beer and felt it move through him like sap through a tree. He grinned.

"We been stalking our quarry," he said. He opened his shirt so that Janet could see the nickel-plated .32 revolver at his belt.

"Jesus Christ," she said. "Is that a real gun?"

Newman opened another beer. He held one toward Hood. Hood shook his head. "Yes, ma'am," Newman said, "it's real. And we have been circling in on old Adolph Karl."

The steaks began to sizzle in the pan.

"Well tell me about it. Tell me everything you've done today. Are you in on this too, Chris?"

Hood nodded. Newman began to slice mushrooms

into the pan with the steaks. "We found out where he lived," Newman said, "and we went and looked it over. We figure we can't get him there so we're waiting to see if he goes out, or goes to work or something like that. We need to get a place where we can hit him and get away clean. It may take some time."

Janet Newman smiled and raised her glass. "Okay," she said. "Home from the hill is the hunter."

Newman smiled back at her. Hood sipped his beer. Newman turned the steaks in the pan with a pair of tongs.

"How long do you think it will take?" Janet said.

Hood shrugged. Newman said, "No way to tell. We'll just have to stay on him and see." He drank more beer and got another can. This time Hood had some too. Janet had another glass of wine. As he cooked, Newman could feel the swell of his biceps tightening his shirt as he bent his arm to move the mushrooms around in the pan. Janet set the table and put a plate of rolls out. Newman put the steaks on each of three plates. His movements seemed precise to him. Controlled. He added steak sauce to the mushrooms and let the sauce cook down a moment in the pan. Then he spooned a serving onto each plate with a spatula. He spilled none. *Good at what I do,* he thought.

As they ate, Newman talked. "We watched that goddamned house all day," he said. "All goddamned day, and nobody stirred."

"Will you go back tomorrow?" Janet said.

"Yeah. He's gotta come out sometime."

"What about your writing?"

"Priorities, lovey. I keep telling you there's got to be priorities. This is life and death. That's number one."

The beer was very cold and tingled in his throat as he drank.

"What made you decide to do it?" Janet said.

"It has to be done," Newman said. "And the . . . the what . . . the insult of it all has to be wiped away. I can't stand to be cowed by those bastards. It's the insult. I just can't accept it."

"Well, I think it's a good decision, whatever reason. I'm proud of you both."

"Wait'll we do it, Janet," Hood said. "We botch it and you won't be proud of us."

"I don't like to think about that," Janet said.

"Well, it's a risk," Hood said, "you have to face that."

"We won't botch it," Newman said. "We must be as smart as these bastards."

"But it isn't just smart," Hood said, "it's also mean. Are you as mean as those bastards?"

"If I have to be. I have always been able to do what I had to do."

Janet nodded. She had finished her steak and was sipping wine. "That's true, Chris. He has always been able to do the things that had to be done."

"I hope he runs to form," Chris said. "There may be some tough things to do. And when we're doing them is not the time to rethink your position on violence."

"I know," Newman said. "I'm committed. I won't back off."

Janet poured more wine. "My God," she said, "isn't it something. Sitting around eating steak, drinking wine, and talking about a killing."

Her face was animated and full of color. *I love the way her lower lip is,* Newman thought. *And how she looks when she's enthusiastic.*

It was nearly eleven when Chris Hood went home. They cleaned up the kitchen together. He locked the doors. And they went upstairs to bed.

"Would you care to have a small screw," she said.

"Don't mind if I do," he said.

"I'll be back soon," she said, and went down the hall to the bathroom.

He loaded the double-barreled shotgun and put it by the bed. He took the .32 off, belt and all, and hung it over the bed post. *Looks like a paperback cover from the forties,* he thought. *My Gun Is Quick.* He liked the way it looked.

He undressed and got into bed. She came back from the bathroom, her makeup off, her face scrubbed. She locked the door behind her and went to pull the drapes closed across the windows.

"Who do you figure will peek," he said. "Somebody up in the church steeple with a spyglass?"

She smiled and pulled the rest of the drapes. Then she turned toward him and stood at the foot of the bed and undressed. The last thing she took off was her underpants, rolling them slowly down across the thrust of her pubic bone and then wiggling them down her thighs until she could step out of them.

The red scratches on her belly were clear. AK. He felt the cortex of desire in his stomach.

She stood still for a moment at the foot of the bed while he looked at her, then she turned off the light and crawled from the foot of the bed up beside him. He shifted over on his right side. She lay on her left facing him. She pulled the covers over them. He put his right hand against the delta where her thighs met. He put his left arm around her and pressed her against him. She kissed him with her mouth open. He put his tongue out, and hers met it at the edge of her teeth and kept his from penetrating. He groaned slightly and pushed his right hand against her. She pressed her thighs together slightly. With her right hand she pushed his hip away slightly and put her hand on his penis. He grunted. She began to move her hand. He groaned. She moved her hand faster. He relaxed the pressure on her vulva, though his hand remained. Her thighs relaxed a little. Her hand moved steadily. He rolled over onto his back, the covers kicked off, moaning steadily, arching his back toward her moving hand, his hand fell away from her body. Her eyes were closed, her face detached and calm. He twisted toward her. She moved her hand faster and he fell back. She rose to a half-sitting position and bent over him. Her back was to his face and arms as she bent over his penis. Lying flat and twisting with sensation he reached toward her but could touch only her back and right hip.

She sat up and lay back. She put her legs apart. He got onto his knees between her legs and she guided him into her. He lay on top of her, one hand holding her buttocks, the other beneath her back, his hand pressing between her shoulder blades. He tried to kiss her. She turned her head away. Her knees were half bent, her eyes closed, she lay quite still as he pumped above her. He put his left hand on her breast, and after a moment she pushed it away. She shifted slightly as his pelvis ground uncomfortably against her. The new position was more comfortable. She grunted once, softly, and put both hands on his rhythmic buttocks.

He ejaculated.

The decrescendo was brief and after a moment as

he lay quietly on top of her, his face pressed in her hair, she made a small hip thrust that told him to get off. As he withdrew she shivered slightly as she always did.

He rolled over on his back beside her, holding her hand. She squeezed his hand, then pulled hers away. And sat up on the edge of the bed.

"I've got to get up," she said. "I'm full of glop."

10

In the morning Janet went to the Boston Public Library and spent the day in the microfilm room reading back issus of *The Boston Globe* for information about Adolph Karl. She went up to the university for her one o'clock class and came back at two-thirty and worked until five. When she got home at six that evening she knew that Karl was married, had two sons, had been in jail for five years on an armed-assault charge, had been arrested four other times for loan sharking and narcotics and had been released. She knew that one of his sons had graduated from B.C. and was now in Suffolk law school. She knew that Karl had a summer home in Fryeburg, Maine. That he like to hunt and fish around Fyreburg, that he was probably active in organized crime, had probably killed four people. She knew that Mrs. Karl's first name was Madelyn and that her maiden name had been Corsetti and that she was active in Roman Catholic women's groups in Lynn and Boston. And she knew that Adolph Karl owned a discount furniture store on Portland Street in Boston.

Her husband and Chris Hood learned of the store

too. It was ten-thirty in the morning when Karl and two other men came out of the house and got into the blue Lincoln with the orange vinyl roof. Hood watched from the seawall and then turned and stared out to sea. Newman started the Bronco and cruised down slowly. He stopped, Hood got in, and they swung out three cars behind the Lincoln.

"He alone?" Newman asked.

"No. There's two men with him. He's in the back seat with one of them. The other one's driving."

The blue Lincoln drove west along the shore drive onto the Lynnway, and south on the Lynnway. It stopped once at a doughnut shop. The man in the back seat got out and went into the shop. Newman pulled the Bronco into a gas station next door and parked by the air hose.

"That Karl?" Hood said.

"No."

Hood got out and put air in the tires. The man came back out of the doughnut shop with a box of doughnuts and a paper bag. Hood got back in the Bronco. The Lincoln pulled back out into the Lynnway traffic, the Bronco fell in behind it. They drove to Boston.

The Lincoln pulled up into a loading zone with a yellow curb and parked in front of a furniture store on Portland Street just up from North Station. The sign said Adolph Karl's Union Furniture. Karl and the two other men got out and went in. Newman drove around the block. On the next pass by Union Furniture the Lincoln was still there.

"Why don't you go in and look around?" Newman said. "I'll keep circling."

Hood nodded. "Let me out on the corner. I'll stroll

in and act like a customer. You go around the block and be on that corner. Double-park there. If I have to come out fast I want to know you'll be there."

Newman said, "I'll be there." He stopped the car.

Hood got out of the car and strolled toward the furniture store. Newman put the car back in gear and went around the block again. He double-parked where Hood had told him to. He could see the front of the store. As he sat, a short fat woman in a tight pink dress that didn't reach her knees shuffled up to the car. She wore blue rubber clogs on her feet. She handed a card through the window of the Bronco. Newman took it. The card said, "I am a deaf mute. You may buy this card for a quarter." Newman dug a quarter from his pocket and gave it to the woman. Her hair was gray and in a tight coil at the back of her head. She wore sunglasses. She took the quarter and moved away up Portland Street, toward Government Center. Newman turned the card over. On the back were diagrams of sign language. *She can tell herself she isn't begging,* Newman thought. He stuck the card in a crack in the defroster vent.

Chris Hood came out of Union Furniture and walked slowly down Portland Street toward Newman. He got in the car.

"Nothing," he said.

"Karl in there?"

"If he was I didn't see him. There were a couple of salesmen. Then there's some stairs along the left wall in the back, and like a balcony of offices across the back on the second floor. I would assume Karl was up there."

"Did it look like a place we could hit him?"

Hood shrugged. "Got to see the upstairs layout. In the store itself it doesn't look promising."

"Do we really need to see upstairs too?"

Hood looked at him for a span of ten seconds. "Yeah, we have to see upstairs. We have to see everything. This isn't Capture The Flag, Aaron. You don't go in unprepared. Here, anywhere. You gotta know what you can expect."

Newman said, "Okay. You're probably right. How we going to do it?"

Hood picked the card off the defroster slot and read it. "First let's park this thing," he said.

Newman found a meter past the store on the right.

"First off, it's gotta be you," Hood said. He put the card back in the defroster slot. "The salesmen have seen me in there. They'll be too suspicious if I'm caught trying to go up to the offices."

Newman felt the fear again. It surged in his stomach and flashed along his arms and into his fingertips. He kept his face still.

"How about I use that card?"

Hood looked at the card again.

"Go in and pretend to be a deaf-mute beggar and go upstairs and wander around?"

"Yes," Newman said. His throat was stiff. "And if anyone catches me I hand them the card."

Hood pursed his lips and raised his eyebrows. "Not bad," he said. "But you look too good."

He reached into the glove compartment and brought out a felt fishing hat. "Try the crusher," he said. "Just put it on and let it be as wrinkled and mangy as it is. Don't smooth it out."

Newman put the hat on. "Okay," Hood said. "And we'll have to do something with the shirt." He took the skinning knife from his pocket and opened the blade. "Mind if I ruin the shirt? I'll cut the sleeves off almost at your shoulders."

"Go ahead," Newman said. His breath was short.

Hood cut the sleeves off. When he finished Newman leaned over and rolled his pants legs up over his ankles. His bare legs were pale above his blue Pumas. He put the deaf-mute card in his hat band.

"I'll go in first," Hood said. "I told them I wanted to shop around and I might be back. Then you come in and head for the back left. You'll see the stairs."

Newman nodded.

"If there's trouble, start yelling. I'll be up in half a second. And don't be afraid to use the gun. That's what you got it for."

"Okay."

Hood grinned. "Okay, I'm going. You come right behind me."

"Okay."

Hood grinned again. Made a thumbs-up gesture and got out of the car. Newman sat in stillness. He felt thick, as if there were insulation around him and reality were distant and unclear. Hood went into the store and Newman got out of the car and went to the store behind him.

The store was shabby and the furniture was cheap and garish, imitation plush in bright reds and blues. Wooden love seats with small print slipcovering that pretended to be colonial. To his right as he went in, Newman had a sense of Hood talking to a salesman. In the far right back corner of the store another salesman bent over a table, writing in a notebook. Newman walked straight to the back left and up the stairs. Nobody said anything. At the top of the stairs there was a balcony that ran off at right angles to the stairs across the back of the store. There were three frosted glass doors at intervals in the back wall of the balcony. The salesman who'd been writing was now out of sight under the balcony, the other was still talking with Hood.

Newman felt disconnected. His jaws hurt and he realized he was clenching his teeth. He relaxed his jaw. He couldn't seem to feel the gun against his groin as he had before. He ran his left hand over the area as if scratching a bite. The gun was there. He waited for the surge of reassurance but nothing came.

Emptily he moved onto the balcony and opened the first glass door. The room was windowless and empty. The only light came through the open door and the frosted glass partition that separated it from the next office. There was a gray metal conference table and five folding chairs in the room. On the table was a newspaper and an empty cardboard pizza box in which a few crusts of pizza remained. Two paper coffee cups were near the box. In the corner of the room there was a stand-up electric fan. There was nothing else in the room.

Newman closed the door as quietly as he could. Every movement he made he had to think of. Nothing was natural. Nothing automatic. He stepped back from the door. There was light in the next office. *I could tell Chris I tried and it was locked and that there was no one up here. I could turn now and go down and out and go home. And be safe.*

He stepped to the next door. There was light behind it. He could hear a voice. From the floor below a voice said, "Hey, what the hell are you doing?"

His fear saved him. He was numb and slow with it

and didn't react. Instead, mindless and terrified he turned the knob and walked in.

Adolph Karl sat at a desk facing the door with his feet up and his coat off talking into the telephone. *I could shoot him now.* To his left, at a small table against the wall, the two men who'd been with him all day were playing cards. In front of each there was a card up and a card down. *Blackjack,* Newman thought.

Karl said into the phone, "Hold on," then he put the phone down on the desk and swung his feet down onto the floor. He looked at Newman.

"Yeah?" he said.

The two men against the wall both turned toward Newman. One stood up and took a gun from under his coat and held it against his leg. The man with the gun had thick lips and a long face. His hair was curly, and his skin was very white. The other man, still seated, was immense.. *Three. hundred. pounds,* Newman thought. His chest was vast. His stomach stretched tight against his white shirt but it looked hard, like a Russian weight lifter's. His shirt sleeves were rolled back two turns over his forearms, and his wrists were as thick as cordwood. He stood up too and took a step toward Newman. He was tall and his back arched slightly. He was clean-shaven and his hair was slicked back and shiny. He looked very clean.

"The man asked you a question, douche bag," he said. Newman knew the voice.

There were no windows in this room either. Just a cinder-block back wall painted yellow. In the left corner a gray metal file cabinet. There was no rug on the floor. The only light was an overhead hanging fluorescent. The huge man took another step toward Newman. The man with thick lips stood without movement, the gun held against his right thigh.

Newman took the card from his hat band and held it out to the big man. The man read it.

"It's a fucking dummy, Dolph," he said. "He's scrounging." The big man handed the card to Karl. Karl read it.

"Throw him the fuck out," he said. He crumpled the card and threw it on the floor. The big man took hold of Newman's shoulder and turned him around.

Karl said, "Tell those fucking assholes downstairs that if anybody comes wandering up here again I'm going to cut their balls off."

The big man held onto Newman's shoulder with his left hand and shoved him out the door. Newman made no resistance. He was afraid he might fall. His legs had no feeling. The big man shoved him along the corridor and down the stairs, moving him faster than he wanted to walk, so he stumbled and had to hold the banister going downstairs. Newman had a sense of Hood's presence to the left of his periphery.

The big man stopped at the front door, opened it, planted his right foot against Newman's buttocks, and shoved him sprawling, face first, into the street. He let the door close.

Newman lay a moment face down on the sidewalk, feeling the roughness of the concrete against his cheek. He felt as if he might urinate right there, lying down on the sidewalk. He was out of there. He was alive. They hadn't hurt him. He'd done it and survived.

He got up and walked down Portland Street to Hood's car. He got in the passenger side and sat as still as he could. His heart thumped in his chest the way it did after intercourse. He waited for it to quiet. He pressed his open hands on the tops of his thighs. His hands felt sweaty and swollen.

Hood came out of the store and walked down to the car. He got in, took the keys from above the visor, and started the car. They drove down Portland Street, away from the Union Furniture Store.

"You all right?" Hood said.

"Sure," Newman said. "Sure."

11

"So how do you get him?" Janet Newman said.

They sat in the Newmans' kitchen with beer and wine and sandwiches.

"We wait," Hood said, "and watch. We'll see the chance. Killing him's easy. Getting away with it is the hard part."

"Janet, you wouldn't believe what it was like to walk in there on them," Newman said. "The guys that tied you up, one was huge and kind of slick-looking?"

"Yes, and the other had thick lips and a long face. We already went through this."

"That was them," Newman said. He drank some beer. "The same ones, and Karl, sitting right there. The same man I saw kill that woman. And I walked right in on them and got away with it."

"But you didn't kill them," Janet Newman said.

There was silence for a moment. Then Hood said, "It would have been suicide, Janet. We agreed before we went in there that Aaron wouldn't do anything but look and get the layout."

Newman opened another can of beer and drank some.

"Bullshit," Newman said. "When I went in Chris said don't be afraid to use the gun. I don't need anyone alibiing to my wife for me, Chris."

Hood shrugged and looked out the big picture window at the back lawn.

"So why didn't you?" Janet Newman said.

"Because I was scared shit," Newman said, "that's why. I was in a fucking trance I was so scared."

"Well, when won't you be scared? How will you do the job if you're in a trance?"

"Janet," Hood said. "There were two other men in there. Three men with five shots is too much. He did the right thing."

"Shut the fuck up, Chris," Newman said. Hood looked at Newman a moment and something stirred in his eyes again. The muscles at his jaw-hinge tightened for a moment and relaxed. "She can think what she wants," Newman said.

"What the hell is wrong with that question," Janet said. "I am simply looking for information. I am not thinking anything. You got in. You had a gun. You didn't shoot Karl. What's wrong with asking why you didn't?"

"If you don't know, I'm not sure I could tell you," Newman said.

"You tell me it was too dangerous, I understand that. I don't want you to get killed. I don't want you to take crazy risks. But how will I know if you don't tell me?"

"Maybe you better do it yourself," Newman said. He took two cans of beer from the refrigerator and handed one to Hood. Hood put it down on the table in front of him unopened. He sipped from the first can he'd taken. Newman snapped the ring tab off the can and threw it hard at the kitchen sink. It missed and skidded along the counter. "Maybe you better get you a gun and get out and have a go at it. Maybe that will be harder than quarterbacking from your fucking armchair."

The flint edge came into her voice, the one that scared him. "Maybe," she said, "maybe I should be involved. Maybe if I'd been there with a gun this would be over now. Chris, can you teach me to shoot?"

"Either one of us can," Hood said.

Newman sat silently looking at the beer can in his hands. His hands were big and muscular and brown. They were callused. He was a skillful man and could do carpentry and mason work and wiring. He had restored most of the old house they lived in.

"Well," Janet said. "I think you should."

Newman got up from the table and walked out of the kitchen, through the dining room, out of the house through the side porch.

He stood in the dark in his driveway under the spread of the three-hundred-year-old maple that shaded their bedroom during the day. His eyes stung again with tears and his face was wet. *Different*, he thought. *In the dark your own land looks different and feels different.* He walked down the driveway and onto the main street. Smithfield was small and had a New England common with a meetinghouse. At night when there were no cars Newman could imagine being back two hundred years when his house was built and Jefferson was president and the Revolution was but recently past. *Am I right? Or is it booze. Why are there always a few beers involved when I get mad at her? Does the beer distort what I hear, or does it*

*break down inhibitions and allow me to say what I'm
too careful to say when I'm stone sober? What did I
say? Actually I didn't say anything. What the fuck am
I mad at? How could she treat me that way? How
could she be so fucking insensitive?*

He walked past the small village shopping center.
His face was still wet with tears. The lights were on in
the shopping center, though the stores were closed. It
would be embarrassing to be seen walking about
crying. He prided himself on the goodness of his marriage and the loving relationship. He would admit no
problems. He crossed the street, out of the light, and
sat on the small curving stone wall that enclosed the
old cemetery. *What fucking difference does it make?
We'll all be in the ground in forty years or so. At dinner with a body of politic worms. All there is is her.*
He dropped his head and felt sorrow saturate him. *It's
her disapproval. I cannot take any hint of disapproval
from her. I want too much. She has to provide the
complete meaning in my life.* Moths fluttered in the
arc of the streetlight. *I've got to separate at least a
little. Like a kid going to kindergarten. It's part of
growing up. Like the girls going to college. I've got to
make her less central.* A fluffy gray cat with a white
saddle walked silently past, jumped the fence into the
cemetery, and disappeared among the stones. *For crissake, I'm doing this for her and she's bitching about it.*
A ten-year-old Chevrolet Impala sedan turned the corner at the common. There were teenage children in
the front and back. One of them yelled something at
Newman. He couldn't make out what it was. "How
about I kill you, kid," he murmured. "Teach you some
manners."

Insects began to swarm about him. *Doesn't take the*

bastards long, he thought. *The ways of the Lord are often dark but never pleasant.* He slapped at a mosquito. *What will I say to her when I go back. Or in the morning. The silence will be awful or the formal courtesy without warmth. I won't apologize, goddamn it, I'm right. She should have been supporting me. She should have been saying, "Oh heavens, don't get hurt, sweetheart. If anything happened to you I'd die,"* that's it. That's what it is. *She's so fucking businesslike and practical. So controlled. Why can't she just now and again be girly-girly for crissake.* He shook his head as the bugs settled on him. He got up from the wall and walked across the street toward the library. *Just like sex, the bastard. "Here"*—in his mind he mimicked her in a high voice—*"here, you lie still and I'll take hold of you here, and rub you there, and—no no, don't touch—and then I'll do this and that and now we're ready I'll put it in." Fuck her.*

He walked back to his house. Chris was gone. The kitchen was picked up. He went up to bed. She was lying on her side with her back to him watching television on the bedside table with a private listening plug in her ear so that there was no way to know if she were awake. She often slept that way, all night with the television going.

He got into bed beside her without touching and lay on his back in the cool silent room. He stifled real crying that came up on him. He stifled it hard by putting the pillow over his face. But he hoped as well "Don't cry, I love you" and pull away the pillow and lean over to him and put her arm around him and say "Don't cry, I love you and pull away the pillow and kiss him, and say "I'm sorry I hurt you. You're everything I ever wanted." But she didn't. He could not remember that she had ever done such a thing, and he wondered why he thought she might, each time. *Twenty-three years you'd think I'd learn something. Know what I could expect and what I couldn't. Jesus Christ, what a jerk I am.*

With an angry effort of will he stopped crying and lay silent and full of pity in the dark room staring at the ceiling, his hands folded on his stomach. His eyes wide open in the dark.

From the window of the room on the ninth floor of the Hyatt Regency Hotel in Cambridge, a man named Steiger looked out at the Charles River and across it at the buildings of Boston University and beyond them at red-brick Back Bay.

Behind him a blond woman with dark eyes lay naked on the bed reading a guide to Boston. Steiger turned to look at her.

"Angie," he said, "if you're going to bleach your hair why don't you do it all over?"

"You know the truth," she said. "Nobody else gets to look."

"Just me," he said.

She smiled. "Just you."

"You want something sent up?" he said.

She shook her head.

"Wine, beer, some hors d'oeuvres?"

"No. Just let me lie here and cool off."

There was a knock at the door. Steiger walked across and opened it. A man handed him a package wrapped in brown paper. Steiger took it silently and closed the door. He came back into the room with the package.

"What's that?" the blond woman said.

"It's a piece," Steiger said. "I don't carry one on airplanes, so they said they'd furnish me one when I got here."

He unwrapped the brown paper. Inside was a shoebox with Florsheim printed on it. He opened the box and took out a handgun wrapped in a blue terrycloth hand towel. He unwrapped the hand towel. The gun was a Ruger Blackhawk in a hip holster. In the shoebox was a box of Remington ammunition, .44 caliber.

Steiger took the gun from the holster, checked that it was empty, tried the action, examined the firing pin and the barrel, spun the cylinder, and nodded once to himself. He put the gun back in the holster, put the holster and gun back in the shoebox, and put the shoebox on the closet shelf.

"Who are you going to use that on?" the blond woman said.

"Guy named Newman," Steiger said. "Aaron Newman. He's a writer."

"What did he do?"

Steiger took off his shirt and hung it carefully on a hanger in the closet. There were two suits in the closet and three pairs of slacks and two sports jackets. Each was hung precisely. Each had space around it.

"He saw something he shouldn't have and they're afraid he might testify."

"You supposed to kill him or just tell him to keep his mouth shut?"

Steiger stepped out of his slacks and hung them over a hanger. He smoothed the crease with his thumb and forefinger. "They already told him to keep his mouth shut," Steiger said. "But now the man is getting worried. He thinks the cops are following him, and he figures maybe he better close any doors he left open before. I guess if he takes a fall on this it will be a big one."

"So you're going to kill whatsisface?"

"Newman," Steiger said. "Yes."

"How long will it take?"

"A week maybe. I like to look everything over before I move. You come into a town and try to whack the guy out first thing, you're not likely to get ahead. I been doing this a long time now and I don't even have an armed assault bust. You know why?"

"Because you're careful," she said.

"And I have never been in the joint since the year I met you. You know why?"

"Because you're careful," she said.

"Right with Eversharp," he said. "Besides, I do it too quick, we don't get to see Boston and have our tab picked up in this hotel. No point rushing things," he said.

He went into the shower. The blond woman read her travel guide. He came out in ten minutes, his body smooth and shiny from the shower, drying his hair with a towel. She looked at him.

"You're really something," she said. "Forty years old and you haven't got two ounces of fat on your body. What did you weigh when I met you?"

"One-eighty."

"What'd you weigh now?"

Steiger smiled. "One-eighty and two ounces."

"Two ounces in twenty-two years. You're beautiful."

Steiger plugged a maroon hair dryer into the outlet over the bedside table and sat on the bed to dry his hair.

"Twenty-two years?" He took a Lucky Strike from a package on the table and put it in his mouth and lit it from a silver Zippo. "Jesus Christ, you were a baby. Ain't that something, twenty-two years."

"I was fourteen," she said. She ran her hand along his thigh. "But not now."

He put one hand on top of hers. "Your book tell you what we're looking at out our window?" he said.

"I don't know," she said. "What's out there."

"Take a look," he said.

She got up and walked to the window. He looked at her naked back as she walked. She was tanned all over. She looked out of the window at the river and at Boston University beyond it.

"It's a school," she said. "Some college, I imagine." She opened the book and looked at it. "It's Boston University, I think."

He shut off the hair dryer and came and stood beside her. Her head did not reach his shoulders. She leaned her head against him. Below on the river a cabin cruiser headed slowly down the river toward the dam and the harbor. Behind it a wide and symmetrical V spread out over the surface of the river.

"I wonder what it would have been like to have gone to college," she said. "You'd have played football and I'd have been a cheerleader. And we'd have learned stuff and could talk about books and . . ." She shrugged.

Steiger held the burning cigarette in his mouth and let the smoke drift up past his dark narrow face.

"We don't need no fucking college, kid," he said. "We got all we need."

"We got each other," she said.

He put his arm around her. "That's all we need, kid. We don't need any fucking other thing else."

"I know," she said. She put her arm around him and they stood looking down at the river as the powerboat moved out of sight and the wave V'd out and disappeared against the shoreline. "I know."

13

"What we need is a sniper gun with a scope," Hood said to Newman. "We got firepower, but it's short-range stuff and we're having trouble getting close."

"You got anything?" Newman said.

Hood shook his head. They had followed Karl to his furniture store again and were sitting in the Bronco parked up the street, eating hamburgers and drinking coffee.

"You'll have to pick one up," Hood said. "There's a good gun shop in Watertown."

"What should I get?"

"Tell them you want something like a Springfield 1903A4. If you can get one, get it. If they don't have one, get something comparable. Tell them you want it for competition, and be sure it's got a scope. Any .30/06-type rifle with a scope will do. Remington, Savage, whatever."

"Okay, I'll go down tomorrow."

"You have an ID card?" Hood asked.

"Yes, I got one when I bought that shotgun I keep."

"That's all you need," Hood said.

They finished the hamburgers. In the back of the Bronco a big fly with a green tail buzzed at the rear window, bumping it again and again.

"Let's look at the alley," Hood said.

"What's down there?"

"How will we know if we don't look?" Hood said. "You have to know everything, Aaron. The layout of everything, where everyone's deployed, all the options."

Newman nodded. "Okay," he said.

They got out of the car and strolled down toward the alley that ran between the furniture store and a restaurant.

"There's got to be some reason for an alley," Hood said. "There must be a door or a ventilator, or windows or something. Otherwise they'd just butt the buildings up together." His eyes moved back and forth across the mouth of the alley. He was moving on the balls of his feet and his fingers drummed very gently but steadily against his thighs.

God, doesn't he love this, Newman thought.

There were three rats in the alley; one was on the ground and two were in the trash barrel that sat outside the back door to the restaurant. The three rats scuttled away as Newman and Hood came down from the street. Besides the trash barrel there was nothing else in the alley. Opposite the restaurant door was an unmarked fire door with metal facing painted beige. Against the back wall of the alley there was an empty wine bottle leaning, and what might have been human feces in the corner.

Hood reached the blank door into the furniture store. He put one hand quietly on the knob and turned. The door didn't open.

"Locked," Hood said.

Newman felt relief move through him along the nerve tracks. "Okay," he said. "Let's get out of this alley."

Hood was looking up at the alley walls. "Wait a minute now," he said. "We haven't looked at everything. Maybe a window, a ledge, you don't know. You have to check everything out."

"Why, Chris?" Newman said, "Why do you have to . . ." Newman saw a darkness between him and the alley mouth. He looked at it. It was the enormous man from Karl's office. He stood perhaps three feet inside the alley, blocking it.

Newman said, "Chris."

Hood, his back turned to the man, looked over his shoulder. He said softly, "Yeah, I see. Don't touch your gun."

The enormous man said nothing. He moved slowly down the alley toward them.

Hood slid the P-38 out of his shoulder holster. He was halfway behind Newman and the gesture was screened from the big man. Holding the gun at his side and behind his thigh, he turned. The big man kept coming.

Newman felt weak. He knew he wasn't. He could bench-press more than two hundred pounds. He knew he was big and strong. But he felt the strength go out of him. His legs and arms felt limp, the muscles flaccid. He was tired. He faced toward the big man, his hands feeling awkward and out of place. Should he put them up like a prizefighter? Hold them waist high and half closed, ready for anything?

The man was upon them. "What are you doing here?" he said.

The voice, Newman thought, *Jesus what a scary voice*. He tried to bunch the muscles in his shoulders to be ready.

Hood stepped half a step forward and brought the Walther out from behind his leg. In a lateral karate-like movement he swung the gun up over the man's shoulder and hit him in the temple with the top of the barrel where the shells eject. It was so quick the big man never moved. The gun made a sound like a mallet hitting a grapefruit, and the man's knees buckled. Hood hit him again on the temple. The sound was squishier. And again. The man began to sag.

Like a Peckinpah movie, for crissake, Newman thought. It was as if the man were too big to fall suddenly. And slowly, as if in slow motion, he went down and sprawled in the alley on his stomach. Blood showed at the temple in a small ooze, there was redness around it.

Hood bent over and took the man's wallet from his left hip pocket. He pulled the man's wristwatch on its expandable bracelet off the man's left wrist. Then with a short jabbing motion of his right hand, the gun still in it, he gestured up the alley. "Go," he said.

Newman first with Hood behind him ran up the alley. Newman didn't slow at the alley mouth but kept right on running. Hood was five steps behind as they reached the car.

"Drive," Hood said, and Newman got behind the wheel, took the keys from over the visor, and started the car. They turned right on Causeway under the MBTA elevated, and left onto the Charlestown Bridge; in City Square, Newman went up the ramp onto Route 93 and headed north.

"He didn't recognize me," Newman said.

"No. Not without your deaf-mute getup," Hood said. "If he had I'd have killed him."

"You sure he didn't?"

"Yeah. I was watching his eyes; he didn't show any sign of recognizing you."

"Lucky," Newman said.

Hood looked at the contents of the man's wallet. "Not much," Hood said. "Two hundred and twenty-eight dollars, and a Massachusetts driver's license. His name is Tate. Gordon Tate. His address is the same as Karl's. He was born in 1940."

Newman took in a deep breath and blew it out. "That was one of the guys from Karl's office, you know. The same one that tied up Janet."

"I know," Hood said. "One thing, Aaron. You shouldn't have run right out of the alley like you did. You come to an alley mouth you stop and see what's out there. Then you move."

Newman was silent as the Bronco rolled through Somerville toward Medford. "I was scared, Chris. I guess I wasn't thinking."

Hood shrugged. Some powerboats rode at anchor in the Mystic River, narrower here by half than it was only a few miles closer to the sea where the bridge arched over it and the cargo ships sailed up it to the pallet docks.

"I wasn't much help to you in the alley, Chris," Newman said.

They went up slightly onto an overpass that crossed the river. "It takes learning, Aaron," Hood said. "You got a little combat experience today, that's all. Wasn't much you needed to do. You spotted him first."

"Why'd you tell me not to touch my gun?"

"Didn't want to spook them if we could help it.

Shooting might bring cops, or bad guys with guns. I don't know. Kill that guy and maybe Karl would get nervous and be too hard to hit. I just wanted to get by without the guns if we could."

Newman nodded.

"Guy was too cocky," Hood said. "Big huge guys like that are sometimes. Doesn't occur to them that they can be taken. He got too close. Should have had his gun out. Shouldn't have gone down an alley with two guys if he didn't. We're not his size, but we're not midgets. He should have noticed that."

"I don't know if not being a midget outside makes any difference," Newman said. "Not if you're a midget inside."

Newman was staring straight ahead as he drove. Hood looked at him and sucked on the inside of his cheeks and said nothing.

14

Lieutenant Murray Vincent sat in his office at 1010 Commonwealth Avenue and fingered a thick collection of computer print-out sheets. He sat square in his chair with both feet flat on the floor and the computer sheets on his spare neat desk. As he went through them he moved his eyes methodically down the names on the sheets, turned a sheet, read the names, turned a sheet, read the names. Occasionally he stopped and went back reading more data on a name he recognized. He did this for an hour and eight minutes. Then he yelled through the open door, "Bobby." A uniformed State Trooper appeared in the door. "Corporal Croft is out on a detail, sir. Sheet says he'll be back in about half an hour."

"Send him in when he gets here," Vincent said.

In half an hour Croft came into Vincent's office.

Vincent said, "Close the door, Bobby."

Croft did. Then he sat in a straight chair beside Vincent's desk.

Vincent handed him a multifold print-out sheet, folded over. There was a name marked in blue pencil. "That a familiar name to you?" Vincent said.

Croft read, "Aaron Newman. Sure. He's the guy that saw Karl kill the broad in Smithfield and then got scared off."

"It appears," Vincent said, "that Newman has purchased a firearm."

"Un-huh?"

"Whyn't you look into it, Bobby."

"You think he's still involved with Karl?"

"Whyn't you look into it and see. See exactly what he purchased, and see if you can figure out why. But don't talk to Newman without first talking to me. Okay?"

"How'd you happen to see this listing?" Croft said.

"I try to thumb through them all each week," Vincent said. He made a small smile.

"All the firearm purchases in the state? Every week?"

"I just sort of scan them."

"No wonder you're a lieutenant and I'm a corporal."

"I take the Commonwealth's money," Vincent said, "I do the Commonwealth's work."

"Amazing," Croft said. "A-fucking-mazing."

"Bob, stop dazzling me with your vocabulary. Go find out about Newman and his gun. Maybe there's something in it for us."

Croft nodded. He took the folded computer sheet and went out.

Vincent took a brown paper bag out of the bottom right desk-drawer. From it he took a meatloaf sandwich with mayonnaise and lettuce, a nectarine, a Santa Rosa plum, half a dill pickle carefully wrapped in foil, two blue-checkered paper napkins, and a wedge-shaped plastic container in which there was a slice of homemade cherry pie. Taped neatly to the pie container with a piece of Scotch tape was a plastic fork. He spread a paper towel on his desk and carefully arranged his lunch on it. Then he took a big blue and white Thermos bottle from the same drawer and took off the cap. He poured skimmed milk into the cap and ate his lunch. He drank some milk and patted his mouth dry with the napkin and opened the pie container. On top of the pie was a small piece of paper with a heart and three kisses drawn on it. He smiled and put the paper in his desk drawer and ate the pie. When he was through he wrapped the plum and nectarine pits, along with the napkins and the plastic fork, in the foil from his pickle. He threw the foil away. He got up and went to the washroom and rinsed out the Thermos and the pie container. He washed his hands and face and went back to his desk. He put the Thermos and the pie container in the paper bag from which his lunch had come, put the bag away in the bottom right drawer of his desk. He took a toothpick from his shirt pocket and cleaned his teeth. Then he took a file folder from his in-basket and opened it and began to make notations in the margin with a blue pencil.

At two-forty Bobby Croft came back into his office and sat down in the straight chair. He took a small notebook out of his inside coat pocket, leafed through it until he found what he wanted, and then looked up at Vincent.

"Ready, Lieutenant?"

Vincent nodded.

"Newman bought a Springfield '03 bolt-action with a scope and a box of .30/06 ammunition. Told the clerk he wanted it for competition."

"Hmm-um."

"Then I went over the BPL and looked Newman up in *Who's Who* and *Contemporary Authors*. No mention of competitive shooting. I called his publisher and asked them if they knew anything about Newman shooting competitively. Said I was doing a story on writers who shoot and hunt for a Chicago magazine. Woman in the PR department said he gave no indication on his author's biog sheet of competitive shooting. No mention of hunting or woodsmanship or anything remotely like it. Said she'd heard him say at lunch he wasn't an outdoorsman. Ridiculed people who were, she said."

"Hmm-um."

"So why's he want the long-range rifle with the scope? I mean, your Springfield '03 isn't the first gun you think of when you go to buy a rifle."

"They were sniper guns in Korea," Vincent said.

"Too long ago for me, Murray. I'll have to trust your word on that."

"They were," Vincent said. "Bolt-action, a lot slower than the M1's for rapid firing, but for sniping they were perfect. You don't need rapid fire for sniping, and they had good range and didn't jam."

"So why does Newman want a sniper rifle? If you wanted something for protection, that's not what you'd get. You'd get a shotgun or a carbine, something like that."

"Right. It's not a common hunting weapon either. Not with the scope."

"Clerk in the gun shop says he made a point of the scope and the range."

"Man buys a sniper gun," Vincent said, "probably wants to snipe."

Croft put the notebook away in his coat pocket and

leaned back in the straight chair and put his hands behind his head and looked at Vincent.

"You think he wants to shoot Karl?"

"You got a better guess?"

"You think he's got the balls?"

"No, but maybe I'm wrong. It's too big a coincidence. Guy sees Karl do murder. Guy goes to testify. Guy gets frightened off. Guy buys sniper rifle." Vincent spread his hands out, palms up. "What else?"

"He might have the balls," Croft said. "He asked what I'd do if my family were threatened. I told him I wasn't sure. I'd have to be in the spot."

"I know what I'd do," Vincent said.

"I told him that too," Croft said.

"What'd you tell him I'd do?"

"I said you'd blow the guy away."

Vincent nodded.

"Maybe he's going to. It's the way a guy like him would go. Long distance so you don't get blood on your jogging shoes."

"He's not a bad guy, Murray," Croft said. "He didn't like getting scared off. It bothered him."

"It should."

"Murray, not everyone is like you. You been doing this, how long, twenty-something years?"

"Twenty-six," Vincent said.

"You're used to guys with guns. You don't have any nerves. This guy's a writer. Biggest showdown he's had in twenty-six years is whether his serve hit the net or not, you know? He might have the balls."

"I hope so."

"So what do we do?"

"Nothing."

"Murray, we have some reason to think that a man might commit murder."

"Nothing," Vincent said.

"Yeah, okay, I won't get hysterical if Adolph Karl gets aced. He can use it. So can the Commonwealth. But what about Newman? He gets mixed up with Karl, a guy like that, they'll mangle him."

"Maybe, and maybe we'll catch them at it. Then we'll have Karl."

"You are a cold bastard, if you'll pardon my saying so, Lieutenant, sir."

"Newman could have given this to us. He didn't. He wants to do it himself, he takes his chances. If he gets Karl, that's good for us, and him. He gets blown up trying, maybe we can make Karl on that. We don't lose either way."

"Suppose he's lucky and gets Karl. Then what? We put him in the house of blue lights for the rest of his life?"

"Maybe we don't," Vincent said.

"One good turn deserves another?" Croft's face was tight.

"Something like that, Bobby. We can't lose on this one."

"Yeah, well, I take the Commonwealth's money," Croft said, "I do the Commonwealth's work." He got up and left.

15

"So why did you take the watch and wallet?" Janet Newman asked.

"Make it look like robbery," Newman answered.

She nodded. "The big one," she said. "Do you think you killed him?"

Hood shook his head.

"I wish you had," she said. "I remember him looking at me."

Newman felt his insides tighten like a fist.

"It's too bad they spotted us, though," Hood said. "It will make things tougher."

"I think it was a mistake to go down that alley," Newman said.

Hood shrugged.

"We didn't learn anything useful," Newman said.

"Couldn't know till we went and looked," Hood said. "It's important to know."

"Why?" Newman said. "Why is it so important? I think we're taking a lot of risks following Karl around."

"There's risks in anything worth doing, Aaron," Hood said.

They were at the kitchen table in what had become a near nightly ritual. Janet would make sandwiches or a pasta. Newman and Hood would bring home some beer and wine. They would sit at the kitchen table in the summer evenings and talk of stalking Adolph Karl.

"You can't do this in complete safety, Aaron," Janet said.

"It's a matter of degree," Newman said. "What Chris said sounds good but it doesn't mean anything."

"You know it does, Aaron. I've read your books, you understand that."

"No, I don't. Not this way. It's like you want to take risks."

"Risks are part of it," Hood said. "If it's worth doing."

"You act like the risks *make* it worth doing."

Janet said, "What do you think we ought to do, Aaron?"

"I think we ought to shoot him as quick as we can and get this over."

Hood smiled. "We agree, Aaron. I think that too, but you need intelligence. You need to know the enemy before you can make a move, and we haven't gathered enough to figure out how to hit him and get this done with."

Newman ate a forkful of pasta with a basil-and-oil *pesto* sauce. He drank some beer.

"I think you ought to try to get him in the woods," Janet said.

Hood said, "Woods?"

Janet nodded. "He's got a summer place up in Frye-burg, Maine. I looked it up on the map. It's south-western Maine, near the New Hampshire border. According to an article in the *Herald American*, April 18, 1976 . . ."

"She's a scholar," Newman said.

Janet went on: "He's a real hunter and fisherman and goes to his place in Fryeburg whenever he can."

"Do you know the address?" Hood said.

"I drove up there this morning. It's about two and a half hours, and I looked him up in the phone book."

"You cut class?" Newman said.

"Yep."

"I wished you'd waited. We could have driven up together and maybe had lunch on the way back and had a nice time."

Janet didn't answer.

"Maybe that's the end to work from," Hood said. "Maybe we should go up there and wait for him to come."

"Fryeburg's awfully small," Janet said. "It would be easy to be noticed."

Newman opened another beer.

Hood said, "We could keep watching him here. I assume if he heads up to hunt and fish we could tell. Rods, gun cases, waders, that sort of thing being loaded into the car."

Newman said, "I'm going up to bed. You folks work this out and let me know."

They both watched in silence as he walked out of the kitchen and up the back stairs.

Janet shook her head.

"He feels bad," Hood said. "He thinks he didn't react well in the alley today."

"He worries an awful lot about things like that," Janet said. "And then he waits for me to make him feel better. And I don't know what the hell to do."

"Nothing to do, I guess. Just let him know you love him. He'll work it through. He's a good man."

"I know. But he's a complicated man and one with ferocious passions. Sometimes I feel . . ." She shook her head again.

"How do you feel?"

"Inadequate to his passions. And that makes me mad. There's a lot of pulling and shoving in our life. And now this. It will be awful for us both if he can't do this."

"If he can't he'll be dead. Maybe all of us. You can't forget that, Janet."

"I know."

"Do you really know? It's easy to forget it sitting here in the kitchen. But we're involved in a very serious undertaking. And if we do it wrong we may be dead."

"I don't forget," Janet said. "I also don't forget what happened to me." Her face was bright as she said it.

"Yeah." Hood smiled briefly. "I guess you don't." He got up and headed for the back door. "I'll come over in the morning when he's feeling better and see if we can work out some kind of plan," he said.

"Good night, Chris."

Hood left. Janet cleaned up the kitchen and turned off the lights and went upstairs. In the bathroom she put up her hair and washed off her makeup and put on her night cream.

When she came into the bedroom he was still awake, lying in bed leaning against a propped pillow, watching the Red Sox game on television with the sound off and listening to the play-by-play on the radio. He didn't say anything as she got into bed and turned off the light on her side.

"Night," she said.

"Night."

"Are you mad at me?" she said.

"No."

"Then why do you sound it?"

"I'm watching the game."

"Oh."

She was quiet.

"I didn't do well this afternoon," he said.

"Chris says you just need experience."

"You ever wonder how that would make me feel?"

"Being scared, you mean?"

"Yeah, being scared. You ever think, maybe, 'Gee the poor guy must be really down and feeling bad, how can I make him feel better?' You ever have any thoughts like that?"

"I don't know what I'm supposed to say."

"Jesus Christ. It's not 'supposed to.' Don't you have any instincts, any fucking heart? Can't you see I'm hurting? Don't you have any impulse to help me. To put your arms around me and say 'I love you. I don't care what you do, I love you'?"

"Aaron," she said. And stopped. And took a deep breath. It shook in a slight vibrato as it went in. "Aaron, grow up."

"What's that mean? Only little kids need love and compassion?"

"I love you. But if you feel bad about yourself and how you acted I can't fix that. You have to fix that."

"While I'm fixing it, it might help to know you're caring about me."

"Aaron, I've lived with you for twenty-three years. Doesn't that suggest I care about you?"

"Sure, you care about me, but not like I care about you. You don't look forward to coming home and seeing me. You don't get a thrill when I walk through the door. You don't get a thrill from touching me."

"And don't you resent it," Janet said. "Don't you take every opportunity to make me feel guilty that I don't feel like you do. Is there only one way to love? Does everyone have to love the way you do or be not loving?"

"How can you love someone and not feel as I do?" he said.

"One can. One does. The trouble with you is that you're over-invested. You dwell on me too much. Every encounter. Every event. Every exchange of words or ideas is charged as if it were a moment of high passion."

"True. I care only about you. I care only for your approval or disapproval. I have achieved an autonomy in my life that only you violate. Only you and the girls, and the girls are growing and going away. Now it's all turned on you. And you're turning out. You're doing committee work and loving it in there in your asshole department with all the asshole academics pretending to care about Chaucer and Andrew Marvell when all they really want is tenure and promotion."

"Aaron . . ."

"I know it's hard. I know you feel the pressure. I try and change. I try and love you less." His voice thickened. "But think what I lose if I love you less. The central meaning of my life. At forty-six I have to change it?"

"Goddamn," she said.

He turned his face away from her.

"We have long periods where it's fine," she said. "What happened?"

He shrugged. His back turned.

"It's Karl," she said. "This thing with Karl is eating us both."

He was silent.

"What is it, about Karl?"

"What do you mean, what is it? The sonova bitch has two goons violate my home and leave my wife tied up nude for me to find. What the hell do you think it is?"

"It's not anger," she said. "You're scared."

"Of course I'm scared. We're trying to kill a professional thug with bodyguards. Only a fool wouldn't be scared."

"No," she said. "That's true, but that's not it. You're scared you'll fail. That you won't be able to act like a man should, you would say, when someone has manhandled his wife and, your phrase, 'violated' his home."

He didn't say anything.

"That's not an unreasonable feeling," she said.

He was silent and motionless, his back to her. The ball game continued.

"I don't blame you for feeling that way."

"Will you, please, for once in your life, just, please, shut the fuck up."

16

"Nice house," Steiger said.

Angie, in a sleeveless lime-green linen dress, tucked her legs under her on the seat of the rented Plymouth and looked at Aaron Newman's two-hundred-year-old house.

"It looks old," she said.

Steiger nodded. "Let's cruise around back," he said. "See what it looks like."

Angie nodded. Steiger put the Plymouth in drive and went around the block. They parked on the street behind Newman's house.

"What town is this?" Angie said.

"Smithfield," Steiger said.

"We ever settle down, I'd like to live like this," Angie said. Her hands were folded in her lap. Steiger's right hand covered both of hers. Neither seemed aware of touching. It was a gesture so fundamental and one that had been made so often that it was unconscious.

"Yeah," Steiger said. "I wonder if he's got an alarm system. Lot of these houses do. Tied into the police."

"Any way you can tell?"

Steiger smiled at her. "I could break in at night and see if the cops come."

She shook her head. "No good," she said.

"True. I'll see about hitting him outside. If it's no good, I'll go in during the day and do it."

"Anyone else there?"

"Wife, I'm told. She works during the day. We'll come out tomorrow and take a look. Then, depending what I see, I'll figure the best time to hit him."

"I hope you don't have to kill the wife too."

Steiger shrugged. "Don't see why I'd need to, I do it right."

"I wonder if they love each other like we do," Angie said.

"Most people don't," Steiger said.

"I know," she said.

Steiger slipped the car into drive and pulled away from the curb. He drove around the block and parked two houses up from Newman's. Steiger reached over and took a road map out of the glove compartment and spread it open on Angie's lap.

"Anyone comes along, they'll think we're lost."

Angie nodded. "You're not going to do anything today, are you?"

"With you here? Have I ever?"

"No. I know. You wouldn't. It was a dumb question."

"Not dumb. You were worried. You had a right to ask. You're never dumb."

A red and white Ford Bronco came down the driveway of Newman's home and turned right onto Main Street. Steiger started the Plymouth.

"That him?" Angie said.

"Yes. In the passenger seat." He drove down Main Street behind the Bronco. When it turned up onto Route 128 he followed.

At the wheel of the Bronco, Hood said to Newman, "We may as well be watching Karl's place while we figure this out." The Bronco went over a small bump in the road and the long guns, wrapped in a blanket, rattled on the floor behind the back seat.

Newman nodded. "Might as well," he said.

"I think Janet's right," Hood said. "The more I think of it, the more I like it. If we can get him isolated up in the woods, we'll have him off his turf and on mine. We'll have no cops to worry about, nobody to see us. We can lay up somewhere and pick him off with the Springfield."

"Why don't we go up there and wait, then?" Newman said. "The more we hang around Karl and his house and his business, the more risk we run of blowing this." The lines that ran from the corners of his nostrils to the edges of his mouth were deep. His eyes looked heavy-lidded.

"I think you're probably right," Hood said. "Let's give it this day to make sure nothing new develops. Then we can go up country and begin to set up."

"Sure."

"I figure," Hood said, "we can rent some kind of cabin or something up there. We'll do it in my name, just in case Karl's keeping an eye on real estate transactions or something."

"Why would he do that?" Newman said.

"Can't tell. These guys are funny sometimes. Might want to keep track of his neighbors—can't be sure. Besides, someone might recognize your name—you're sort of famous, you know—and talk about it in front of Karl or one of his men."

"Yeah," Newman said, "you're probably right."

"I am," Hood said.

"But maybe you better use a false name too. I mean, if we do hit him up there we'd want to leave promptly, wouldn't we, and not be connected with the area in any way."

"Good," Hood said, "good idea. I wasn't thinking. We'll do it that way. I'll take care of that." He exited Route 128 for Route 95 North. "In fact," Hood said, "why not do it now? Why not drive up there now and take a look around and maybe set up a cabin or something?"

"Better than sitting around waiting for Karl to spot us. Or the giant," Newman said. "He knows our faces. He'll remember us next time."

Steiger turned off onto Route 95 behind them. "If they keep going straight for very long I'm going to drop them," he said to Angie. "I don't feel like driving to New Hampshire, or Maine, or wherever the fuck they're going."

Angie leaned her head against his arm. "Okay by me, I'm getting hungry anyway."

"We'll keep an eye out for someplace," Steiger said. "If they just keep driving we'll stop for lunch. I'm not going to hit him today anyway."

Angie smiled.

At Portsmouth Circle the Bronco headed northeast on Route 16. Steiger swung off of the highway and followed a sign that said "Portsmouth Downtown."

"Look in your guidebook, Angie," he said. "See what's a good place to eat in this town."

17

"Did you know that Chris prowls around our yard at night?" Janet said.

Newman shook his head. "What do you mean prowls around?" he said.

"I got up about four in the morning a couple of days ago and looked out the bathroom window and he was standing under that big white pine tree in the back, with a rifle. And I thought, 'What the hell is he doing?' And so last night I was up till about two doing some stuff for the affirmative action task force and I thought, 'By God, I'm going to check.' So I turned out the lights and went and looked out all the windows and he was there. He was out front, in the bushes between us and the Frasers."

They were lying together in bed. Newman was reading the book review section of last Sunday's *New York Times*. Janet was watching the Johnny Carson show. Her hair was in rollers, a blue kerchief tied around it. She had on pajama bottoms and an old white shirt of Newman's. There was cream on her face.

"That figures," Newman said.

"Is he guarding us?"

"Yeah, partly. But he's playing too."

"Playing?"

"Cops and robbers. Cowboys and Indians. The Lions and the Packers. Rangers and gooks. I think this is a kind of game for him. It's the most fun he's had since he got cut by the Lions."

"What could be fun about standing around in the dark all by yourself all night. When does he sleep?"

"He told me once that he only slept three or four hours a day. Always been that way, he said. And it is fun to be a guard. Or at least it's fun for a little while and if you're a certain kind of guy. Think of the high points in his life."

"Football and Korea," Janet said.

"Combat, in a sense."

"Yes. He does karate too, doesn't he?"

"Black belt."

"Formalized combat."

"And since he was cut by the Lions, how have things been going for him?"

"Not good," Janet said. She had turned the sound down on the remote control mechanism by her bed. On the screen Robert Goulet sang soundlessly. "He hasn't been very successful or made very much money. His marriage didn't work. I don't know how the new place is doing, do you?"

"He doesn't talk about it," Newman said.

"So you're saying," Janet said, "that this situation came along and gave him a chance to do something he's good at, and to feel good about himself." She had turned on her left side, facing Newman, and rested her head on her propped left elbow.

"A chance, as the jargon would have it, to maximize

his potential. I mean, for crissake, he's the Michelangelo of *machismo* and for twenty years there's been little call for it from the society he moves in."

"So he can stand out there with his rifle, the silent protector. Tireless, brave, deadly. Yes. I see."

"I think so," Newman said. "I don't mean to put him down. We need him badly in this. And he is tough. Toughest bastard I ever knew. And it's comforting to know he's out there. But he's also beginning to scare the shit out of me."

"You think he takes too many chances?" she said.

"I think he doesn't want this to end," Newman said. Janet thought about that as she looked at her husband. Behind her the voiceless Carson show ended and Tom Snyder appeared.

"That would make sense," she said. "If it ended he'd be back at his restaurant doing what he was doing, nothing bad. But nothing exciting. Nothing that engages his, what, physical self? Beyond throwing out an occasional drunk."

Newman nodded. "I think if he really wanted this finished we could have done it already. I think it could be over with. But Chris. 'Let's check down this alley,' he says. 'Let's take another look at his house.' We go over it and over it. We plan and talk. 'You can't know too much,' he keeps saying. And I'm afraid he's going to get us killed."

"Jesus," she said. "All this time I've been feeling better about it all because Chris was involved. You think it's worse?"

"It's both," Newman said. "I don't know if I could do it alone. But Chris's goals aren't the same as mine. I mean, I want this over. I can't write. I'm scared all the time. I worry about you. You know what we're doing tomorrow? We're going to get outfitted for the woods. We spent most of Tuesday finding a spot to stay near Fryeburg and surveying the area. The spot to stay took an hour. The rest of the afternoon and evening we checked the cabin where Karl stays. Looked at the woods, walked ridge lines." Newman shook his head. "Goddamn," he said.

"What are you going to do?"

"Christ, I don't know. Even if I could do it without him, how could I tell him to screw? He's already risked his life for me. He's in a conspiracy to murder. If we get caught he's an accessory even if he bails out now. And this is the biggest thing in his life. How can I tell him we don't want him? That he's counterproductive?"

"I know. I couldn't say that to him either."

"What would help, would be if you came with us."

"You mean to Maine?"

"Yes, and stayed right with us through the actual shooting and everything."

"I'm not saying I won't," Janet said, "but why?"

"It would help control Chris. He'd feel protective of you, because you're a woman, and it would give me courage. I'm much braver with you than I am alone."

"Do you worry about my safety at all?"

"Yes," he said. "But I'm trying to really look at things. I'm trying, as someone suggested recently, to grow up. This is life or death. I can't romanticize. I need you. There's risk to you but I can't make it without you. I know it, and I'm willing to risk you to help me through this. It's not a posture I'm proud of, but there it is."

She said nothing for a long time. On the television

Tom Snyder threw his head back in pantomime laughter.

"Yes," she said, "I'll go. I want to go. I am not afraid. I would kill Karl in a second and never feel a thing. It's my problem as much as yours. But I want you to teach me to shoot."

Newman wasn't looking at her now. He was staring at the silent television. "Yes," he said. "I'll teach you. It's easy. You just point the gun and pull the trigger. Just like the movies. You can learn easy."

"Okay," she said.

"Are you mad?" he said.

"I don't know," she said. "I want to go to sleep now. I have an early class, I have to get some sleep. I didn't get to bed till three last night."

"But you don't think I'm that swell to ask you to go, do you?"

"It doesn't matter. I said I would."

"But it matters if you think badly of me."

"I don't think badly of you."

"But you're mad."

"I'm getting mad, Aaron. I said I'd do it, now let me alone. I want to sleep."

She turned away from him, shut off the bedside light, shut off the television, and shrugged the covers up over her shoulder, settling her head on the pillow.

The twisted knot in his stomach that had been there since he'd seen the murder twisted a little tighter. He shut off his light and lay on his back and felt it tighten.

Outside, in the shadow of now green forsythia bushes, along the fence Chris Hood squatted with the Ithaca pump gun across his thighs and looked carefully at the yard and empty street. Then he moved silently toward the backyard, staying close to the bushes, the shotgun butt braced on his hip, looking slightly sideways so as to see better in the dark. He was dressed in black and had put burnt cork on his face. On his belt, at the small of his back, was a bowie knife with a nine-inch blade.

In the backyard he stood motionless and nearly invisible in the shadow of an old sugar maple, and watched the house, barely breathing, listening for enemy footsteps.

18

"During the day he's always with his buddy," Steiger said. "The lights stay on at night usually till midnight, one o'clock. If there's an alarm, they normally would turn it on when they went to bed. Otherwise they'd keep tripping it, letting the cat out, dumping the garbage, that kind of thing. Embarrassing as hell when the cops come running in with the blue lights going and the weapons out and it was you throwing out the coffee grounds."

As he talked Steiger was looking out the hotel window at the Charles, dark now and glossy-looking with the lights reflecting off of it from Storrow and Memorial drives. Angie sat with no clothes on at the round table on which they ate breakfast, and did her nails.

"So when would be best?" Angie said.

"In about an hour," Steiger said. "Round ten o'clock. I go to knock on the door. When he answers I do it, and leave. Tomorrow we go back to Cleveland."

"You're going tonight?"

"Yeah."

"I hope you don't have to kill the wife."

"If she doesn't see me, I won't. If she does, I will. It's luck."

"I know," Angie said. "You want to make love again before you go?"

"Whatever we do together is making love, Angie." He walked over from the window and touched her shoulder. "We're making love all the time."

"Okay," she smiled. Her nails were done.

"If anything happens to me you know what to do?"

"Like always. Every time you go out you go through it with me. I have the safe-deposit key. I've got plenty of money to get home. I leave everything here and go."

"Good. Kiss me good-bye."

She stood and pressed against him and kissed him, careful all the time that her still wet nails didn't touch his clothes.

"Hurry back," she said.

"I always do."

Steiger took the shoebox from the top shelf of the closet. He took out the Ruger, loaded it, put the holster on his belt, slipped the nose of it into his back pocket. He took twelve rounds of .44 ammunition, wrapped six in a Kleenex and put them in the left shirt pocket of his tan Levi's shirt. He wrapped six more in another Kleenex and put them in the right shirt pocket. He buttoned both pockets. He put on a dark blue summer-weight blazer with plain brass buttons. It covered the gun. He slipped a package of Lucky Strikes into the breast pocket of the blazer, adjusted his shirt collar in the mirror so that the points of the collar rolled out over the lapels of the blazer. He looked at his watch.

"Okay, babe. See you pretty quick. How about late supper in the room when I get back?"

"Wine, cheese, French bread, and a pâté?"

"Wonderful."

He went out of the hotel room and took the elevator to the lobby. The elevator was glass-walled and the lobby was eleven stories high. He looked down, as the elevator descended, at the fountains on the ground floor. The elevator seemed to descend into them.

He went to the hotel garage, got the rented Plymouth, paid the Puerto Rican attendant at the gate, and drove out. On Memorial Drive he turned left and headed east along the river. At the end of Memorial Drive he turned right across the Charles River Dam, past the Science Museum, stopped for the lights at Leverett Circle, and then cruised up the ramp to the expressway and headed north up Route 93. As he drove he turned the tuning dial on the radio until he found an easy-listening station. He listened to the music as he drove toward Smithfield. He was listening to the orchestra of Frank Chacksfield as he turned off Route 93 at the 128 exit and went north on Route 128. He was listening to Carly Simon as he reached the Smithfield exit and turned off. As he came into the center he turned the radio down. He parked on the street in front of the home next to Newman's. Hanging from a colonial lamppost by the front gate a small white sign with pseudo-rustic ragged ends said *The Frasers* in brass letters.

Steiger left the keys in the ignition, left the parking lights on, and got out of the car. He closed the door quietly and walked briskly back toward Newman's house. It was set back from the street, and the front yard was shadowed by old maple trees grown huge over several centuries. He turned without any hesitation into the long driveway smelling of bark mulch and walked toward the side door of the house. The lights were on in the house, in most rooms. Upstairs and down. He took the Ruger out of his hip holster as he walked up the drive, and held it against his leg.

When Steiger reached the side door Hood stepped out of the shadowed bushes behind him and jacked a shell into the breech with the pump action of the shotgun. Steiger turned at the sound. The .44 still held against his right leg, his face was inquisitive.

"What the hell is this," he said.

Hood said, "Don't bullshit me, Jack. I saw you take the gun out coming up the drive." He held the shotgun steady on Steiger's middle. "Reach across with your left hand. Take the gun by the barrel. Hold it by the barrel and toss it with your left hand over here to my right. You do anything quick and I'll cut you in two."

"You got the cannon," Steiger said. He tossed the gun left-handed and butt-first onto the bark-mulch-covered driveway near Hood's right foot. His face was still pleasant and quizzical.

With the shotgun steady still on Steiger, Hood felt with his foot for Steiger's gun in the driveway. When he found it he maneuvered it into position and then kicked it into the bushes with his heel. "Put your hands on top of your head," he said to Steiger. Steiger did, not clasping them together but resting the right lightly on top of the left.

Hood stepped closer to search Steiger for a gun. He held the shotgun against Steiger's neck as he patted him down on the left side, then he switched the shotgun from right hand to left so that he could search

Steiger's other side. Steiger brought his right elbow around and hit Hood on the temple as the gun was in mid-switch. Hood staggered and dropped the shotgun.

Steiger bent down for it and Hood kneed him in the face. It straightened Steiger up but he had the shotgun. Hood lunged in against him, locking his arms around Steiger's. The shotgun was in Steiger's right hand but he couldn't turn it to bear on Hood. The muscles in Hood's back and shoulders swelled with effort as he clamped his arms tighter around Steiger, his balled right fist pressing into the small of Steiger's back, his left hand covering it, adding pressure. With his hands he pulled in and up, leaning his chest into Steiger, bending him back while keeping his arms pinned against him. Hood's neck thickened, the trapezius muscles bulged up at the base of his neck and across his shoulders. Steiger tried to use the shotgun butt against Hood's kidneys, but it was too awkward an angle to hurt. In his present position the shotgun was useless. He dropped it and locked his own hands behind Hood's back. Hood had arched forward in arching Steiger back and thus had an advantage in leverage. Steiger couldn't reverse it, he was bending farther back and it was harder to breathe. He let go of Hood's back and brought his hands down under Hood's buttocks. He got hold and heaved back. Hood's feet came off the ground. His leverage was lost. Steiger was able to straighten his back and turn Hood toward the house. He tried to ram Hood against the cement stairs to the porch door but he couldn't and they both fell and rolled, locked in each other's embrace, fifteen feet down the driveway. Hood released his hold as they rolled and came up on his feet under the huge old maple tree. Steiger came up opposite him. Steiger's gun was somewhere in the bushes. Hood's shotgun was fifteen feet away back up the driveway. Steiger hit Hood a sharp left-hand hook on the right cheek and followed with an overhand right that staggered Hood against the tree. He kicked at Hood's groin, but Hood karate-blocked it with his left forearm. Hood reached behind him with his right hand and brought out the bowie knife. It was dark but there was enough light filtered in from the street lamps to see the knife. Steiger backed away, Hood followed. Hood held the knife low in his right hand, sharpened side up, moving it back and forth in front of him. His knees were bent and he shuffled like a boxer, left foot always ahead of the right. Steiger, as he backed away, kept his hands out in front of him, overlapping the thumbs, making a V and aiming the crotch of the V at the bowie knife as it moved. Hood had both hands on the knife, ready to switch to either hand if Steiger went for one. They were in the shaded darkness under the big maple tree as they moved down the sweet-smelling bark-mulch driveway. A car went by on the street behind Steiger. Neither Hood nor Steiger knew. Both concentrated on the knife. Nothing else impinged, nothing else was real. Their faces were serious. Steiger took a head-jerking glance at his car parked in front of the next house. It was too far to run. The knife would catch him before he could get in and lock the door. He half-turned as if he would, and as Hood charged he gave him a head fake and dashed for the shotgun, past Hood, back up the driveway. Hood caught the back of his jacket as he went by. He half-turned him and drove the nine-inch knife blade upward into Steiger's stomach, turned it at the end of the thrust, and pulled it toward him along the line of Steiger's rib cage. Steiger made a soft sound, Hood pulled the knife free and slashed it back and across Steiger's throat. Steiger fell down and died on the bark mulch in silence.

19

"You mean the bastard is lying out there in the driveway, now?" Newman said. He wore a green velour bathrobe and no shoes.

Hood said, "Yes. We'll have to do something with him."

Janet said, "There's that big roll of polyethylene in the shed. You could wrap him in that if he's messy."

"I'll get it," Hood said. "You get dressed, Aaron, and help me."

"I'll come too," Janet said. Hood looked at her for a moment and then went to the shed.

When Newman and his wife came out of the house Hood had spread a large sheet of polyethylene on the ground beside Steiger's body.

"Help me roll him onto it," he said.

Janet looked away but knelt down beside Hood. Newman hesitated, then crouched down beside them. They rolled Steiger's body over, onto the polyethylene.

"You got some tape or something?" Hood said.

Newman said, "I'll get some." He got up quickly and went to the house. Hood and Janet folded the polyethylene carefully around Steiger's body. Janet kept her head averted all the time she worked, looking only obliquely at the corpse in front of her.

Newman came back with a large roll of gray duct tape. They taped the polyethylene wrapping around the body.

"We'll put it in my Bronco and take it someplace and dump it."

"Where?" Newman said.

"Wherever we can, away from here," Hood said. "You don't want to explain this to the cops."

"You think it's one of them?"

"I should think so. I figure they decided to hit you," Hood said. "I was afraid they might so I staked you out."

"It has to be," Janet said. "It's too huge a coincidence any other way."

"That means there may be another one coming."

"Not if we get to Karl first," Hood said. "If he's dead there's no reason to kill you."

"Unless they suspect me of doing it," Newman said. He felt sick and very weak. It was hard to keep his shoulders straight.

"Well, first we have to take care of this," Janet said. "I think we ought to put him in the trunk of his car and put the whole thing, car and body, where it won't be found."

"The car," Hood said, "Jesus, I forgot about his car. Good you remembered, Janet."

"Where can we put it where no one will find it, where they'll just disappear?"

Hood was silent.

Newman said, "The airport. You drive in, take a ticket, park the car, lock it, take the keys, and walk right into the airlines. We can pick you up like you were just coming in. Right in front of American on the arrivals level. Ground floor, you know?"

"Not bad," Hood said. "People leave cars there like that for weeks. By the time he's found we'll have done Karl in. I'll see if the keys are in the car. If they are I'll back it in here."

"And if they aren't?" Newman said.

"We'll have to unwrap him and find them."

"Oh, Jesus," Newman said.

Hood walked fast to the rental Plymouth. He got in and started up and drove past Newman's driveway and stopped and backed up and swung in. He stopped under the tree and got out. They loaded the body in the trunk. Janet and Newman took the feet, and Chris handled the head and shoulders. After they closed the trunk Hood said, "I'll need some gloves." Janet nodded and went to get them. While he waited Hood carefully wiped off the trunk and the door and the steering wheel with his handkerchief.

"I'll drive it," Hood said. "You follow me and drive me home."

"Leave it in the airport garage," Newman said. "And then walk into the terminal and we'll pick you up outside American Airlines like you were arriving."

"Okay," Hood said. "That's good. We'll lock his gun in the trunk too. Don't want to get caught with it."

Janet went for gloves. Newman got a flashlight from the kitchen drawer and found Steiger's gun in the bushes. He didn't touch it. He waited for Hood to come with the gloves on. They were leather work gloves with a drawstring that had a red ball on the end of the drawstring. Hood picked up the gun and put it in the trunk of the rental Plymouth and got into the driver's seat.

"Meet me in a half hour at American Airlines," he said.

Newman nodded. "Okay, Chris," he said. "I know you saved my life tonight. And I know this is dangerous, what you're doing now . . ."

"Don't worry about it, just meet me at American. I'd hate like hell to have to get home by cab."

He started and pulled the Plymouth away from the curb. Newman got in his own car with Janet and drove after him.

It was after midnight and cool for late summer. The top was off Newman's Jeep and the open air was a bit uncomfortable.

"There's spare jackets in the waterproof bag back of the seat," Newman said. "Want one?"

"Yes, I'm freezing."

Newman stopped and got two terrycloth-lined vinyl slicker jackets out of the bag behind their seats. He gave the smaller one to Janet and put on the bigger one. They were bright orange.

"Thanks for coming," Newman said.

"If that was one of them, and it must have been, we've got to get out of here tomorrow. When he's found, someone will come again. They'll have more reason to be angry. They'll assume you killed their first man."

"I know."

"We'll go up to Fryeburg and wait until Karl comes and we'll kill him quick and then it will be over."

20

"That's Karl's place there," Hood said to Janet. "On the island." The three of them stood on the small patio of a rented summer home and looked out over a lake. Janet was looking through binoculars.

"All I can see is the dock," Janet said.

"The cabin is in the woods," Newman said. "At night you can see the lights."

"Any way to get there besides boat?"

"No."

"He the only one on the island?"

"Yes."

Behind them their cottage was weathered shingles, with aqua shutters and trim. Living room, kitchen, bathroom, two bedrooms. It stood at the end of a half-mile dirt driveway that branched from a two-mile dirt road. Below them was the lake. The banks were ten feet high. A footpath had been cut in and steps made with short lengths of log. The path led down to a dock and a float. An aluminum canoe was moored to the float.

"Is that our canoe?" Janet said.

"Yes. It goes with the rental."

"What names are we using?"

"Marsh," Hood said.

Janet nodded. "Well," she said, "let's get unloaded."

"I'll do that," Hood said. "Why don't you folks take a walk. I'll set up here."

"Don't be silly," Janet said. "We'll help."

"No, I'd rather, really. You and Aaron take a stroll around and see what the situation is. Better take a gun. I'll set this up."

"Yeah, okay," Newman said. "I'll give Janet a shooting lesson."

"No gunshots, though, just snap her in."

Newman nodded.

"This is ridiculous," Janet said. "Why should he . . ."

Newman shook his head. "Come on," he said.

They got the M1 carbine and a full fifteen-round clip from the Bronco and walked up the dirt driveway.

Newman said, "Don't you see he's setting up a command post?"

"A command post?"

"Yeah, for the search-and-destroy operation. If we were around we'd spoil it."

"Ahh."

"Yes. When we get back he'll have it all ready for all emergencies."

"Okay," Janet said. "Let's find a place to practice with the gun. What's 'snap in'?"

"You pretend the gun is loaded and you practice shooting it, but because it's empty when you pull the trigger it just snaps. They used to do it in basic training."

At the end of the driveway they turned right and walked along the dirt road dappled by leaves and sunlight, silent in late summer.

Behind them, at the cabin, Hood began to unload the Bronco. First he brought in the guns: the Ithaca 12-gauge, the Springfield with the scope, the Winchester, and the handguns in a red and white gym bag that said Speedo on the side. He took out the .45 and a shoulder holster, slipped into the holster harness, checked the clip in the butt of the .45, and slid the gun into the holster under his left arm. He piled the rest of the guns on the couch. Then he went back to the car and carried everything into the house and put it in the living room on the floor.

They had brought food in an old green cooler: beer, bourbon, cheese, fruit, some steaks. He put the food in the refrigerator. From a cardboard carton he took bread, peanut butter, crackers, granola bars, baked beans in cans. He put two sleeping bags in one bedroom and a single sleeping bag in the other. From a tackle box he took ammunition for the guns. On the large dining table in the living room he lined up the guns, and beside each one he put its ammunition. There were three pistol belts. He put the two remaining handguns into holsters and attached them to the pistol belts. On one he put a knife, on the other a hatchet. On the third belt he put the bowie knife and a hatchet in its case, and strapped on the belt.

On the floor beneath the table he put three flashlights, three waterproof containers of matches, three light nylon knapsacks, three nylon pullovers. He picked one up, slipped into it, pulling it down over his head. He tried to get the .45 out of its shoulder holster. He couldn't. He removed the jacket, took off the shoulder harness, slipped the .45 into a regulation holster, attached it to the pistol belt. Then he took off the belt, put the pullover back on, strapped the pistol belt around his waist. The gun was at his right, the hatchet on his left side. Hanging from the belt in the middle of his back was the knife. He looked at his reflection in the window, then went to the bathroom and looked more carefully.

In a clearing, up an old logging road, with insects humming softly and often biting, Aaron and Janet Newman stood side by side. She held the empty carbine.

"Slide the bolt back," he said.

"Show me," she said.

He took the weapon. "See," he said, "this little tit here, you push it back with your left hand, like this." He slid the bolt back and let it snap forward.

"Why do I do that?"

"In this case, to see that it's not loaded. If the clip were in it would jack a shell up into the firing chamber and cock the gun."

He pulled the trigger and the hammer snapped down on the empty chamber. "Okay," he said, "you do it."

She took the gun and pushed the retracting handle on the bolt back. She let it go and it slid forward. Then she pointed the gun and pulled the trigger. Snap.

"Good," he said.

"Why don't I hold it in the other hand and push the whosis back? It's awkward to reach across like that."

"Bolt," he said. "Because then you'd be holding it left-handed, and you don't want to. You are right-handed and want to be ready to shoot and not switch the thing back and forth. You can do it like this too, if you want to."

He held the butt of the carbine against his thigh, his left hand on the stock forward of the trigger housing. With his right he snapped the bolt back. He snapped the trigger and handed the gun back to her. She tried running the bolt back as he'd shown her.

"I like the first way better," she said.

"Okay, but make sure, whichever way, that you don't end up trying to shoot left-handed."

"Okay. What next? Pretend it's loaded. I run the whosis back."

"The bolt," he said.

"The bolt. I run the bolt back and let it go forward. Then I aim it." She put the carbine to her shoulder. "And pull the trigger."

"Good," he said. "I don't know how you'll be shooting. If it's at close range and sudden, you'll shoot any way you can. Otherwise you may as well learn the right way." He took the gun.

"Get it against your shoulder, then hold it with your left hand and reach up with your right toward the sky, like this, and then keep your elbow pointed up and reach down and grip it with your right hand like this. You don't want your elbow down in against you like this. You want it up and out like this."

"It looks awkward," she said.

"A little, but be comfortable, don't strain, just keep the elbow out and up as much as you can. Move your left hand down the stock a little farther. No, toward the front. Good."

"Now I shoot?"

"Not yet. Pick out something, a leaf, a rock, whatever. Aim the gun so the leaf or whatever it is sits on the sight, in between the two outside wings and on top of the center thing. You see? See it? How if you get it right it sits up there, almost seems to magnify?"

"Okay."

"Now breathe out, and don't inhale. Aim, take up the slack in the trigger, now squeeze the trigger, slowly." Snap.

"Can I inhale?"

"Yes. The Army had a little code for it you could say to yourself: BASS. Breathe, Aim, Slack, Squeeze. Don't jerk the trigger, *squeeeeeze* it, you know?"

She nodded. "Then I push the whosis back?"

"Bolt," he said. "No. From there on until the gun is empty you just keep pulling the trigger. The explosion of the weapon will push the bolt back and eject the spent shell and put a new round in the chamber and cock the hammer."

"So, pretend it's loaded, I slide the thing back. Breathe, Aim, Slack, Squeeze." Snap.

She repeated the process several times.

"I think she's got it," he said, "by God, I think she's got it."

"Let me practice putting the clip in."

"Doesn't matter," he said. "I'll put it in for you when you need it."

"I want to know how myself, Aaron."

"Oh, for crissake."

"Aaron, I have to be able to do it if you're not there."

He took the clip out of his pocket and looked at her for a long time. "Yes," he said. "Of course you do. I might get shot. You might be alone."

The hum of the insects was steady in the clearing. More of them now that the sun was going down. They buzzed and bit, and both Newman and Janet waved them away automatically and almost continuously.

"You just slip it up in, like this. Then slap it home. Just make sure the bullets are pointing in the right direction, the barrel end, not the stock. To release it you press this little buttonlike, here."

She did as he said.

"You remember all this from the Army?" she said.

"Yeah. They have an excellent pedagogical technique. They threaten you and they mean it. Fear is underrated as a motivator."

She smiled. "Isn't that what's motivating us?"

"Yes," he said. "It surely is."

21

"I was in town," Hood said, "while you were out firing, and I picked up some more supplies."

"We weren't actually firing, Chris, we were just snapping the hammer."

"You know what I mean," Hood said. "Now here's how I've set things up. The guns are all loaded, so be careful. There's a long gun and a handgun for each of us. Janet gets the carbine and the .32, they're the lightest weapons. I'll take the Springfield and the .45; Aaron, you get the Winchester and the P-38. I've also organized three knapsacks. In each one there's a dozen granola bars, matches in waterproof wrap, extra ammo for both guns, but only for your own so you have to keep the sacks straight. I've put our names on them."

Newman looked at the green nylon knapsack. Across the back, between the padded straps, it said Aaron in black ink.

"I used indelible ink so it wouldn't run if we sweat. There's also a roll of nylon cord, a roll of toilet paper, a small first-aid kit, a flashlight, and a down vest. The vest is rolled up inside the nylon pullover parka. In the late summer it gets cold up here at night, and maybe you'll need it. You should put in some dry socks and clean underwear, or whatever you might want. But this is for emergencies, so you don't want to travel heavy. Anything I forgot?"

"If it's an emergency," Newman said, "you better put in more toilet paper. I may shit myself."

Hood shook his head. "Don't kid around about this, Aaron. You've got to be ready, and you've got to cover everything. You should always be wearing clothes you'd be willing to live in in the woods. Jeans, boots, good shirt. If your feet get wet, change at once, get into dry socks, never get caught. You can't tell when we'll have to move sudden."

"How about insect repellent," Newman said.

Hood stood motionless. "Jesus, I'm slowing up. Yeah, of course, insect repellent. I got some in town." He went to the kitchen and returned. "How the hell could I have forgotten that?" he said. "Here, I'm putting one in each bag."

Newman looked at the three knapsacks laid out neatly, the three long guns to the right of each knapsack, the three pistol belts rolled and laid out to the left of each knapsack.

"The small first-aid kit in each bag contains bandages, antiseptic, some aspirin," Hood said.

"Chris, that's wonderful," Janet said. "You've thought of everything."

"I don't like forgetting the bug dope," Hood said. "I shouldn't forget anything."

"How about a canteen?" Newman said.

"No need," Hood said. "The lake's drinkable, and there's a lot of streams, and the Saco River runs clean here. Canteen just weigh you down for nothing."

Hood wore hiking boots, Levi's jeans, and a tan Levi's work shirt. As he talked he stared out the living room window toward Karl's camp on the island a half mile away. It was nearly dark and some light showed through the trees from the cabin. Hood picked up his pistol belt and strapped it around his waist. "It would make sense if we wore these all the time. Be ready in case we're surprised. We won't be . . ." He thought for a minute, couldn't find the right word, shrugged, and said, "You know."

Newman picked up the other two belts. He handed one to Janet and put the other one on. "Here," he said to Janet, "you adjust it this way. See, you slide this along then put the little hook in here." Together they adjusted the pistol belt. The .32 looked somewhat undersized on the broad web belt.

"Pistol-packin' momma," Newman said.

Janet smiled. Hood stared steadily out the window at the lights on Karl's island.

"Tomorrow," Hood said. "Tomorrow we'll set up a shooting spot and watch the island all the time, take turns. They have to row out there, and we should have a nice clean shot at them when they do. And remember, when we do it, then we get in the car and go. We keep all our clothes and stuff in the car. When we go we take the guns, the bedrolls, and the knapsacks, and drive away. The minute we stop shooting."

Newman nodded. "Yeah, we got it. We went over it all driving up, Chris."

"Does it hurt to run through it to remind us, Aaron?"

"No."

"Okay."

Janet said, "Why don't we grill some steaks over the

fire? They've got one of those swing-out grills, built in."

"And a few beers," Newman said, "here in the great outdoors. I'll get a fire going."

"You do that," Hood said. "I'm going to look things over a little." He went out through the screened side door, across the small patio, and disappeared without a sound into the tall trees at the edge of the cabin clearing.

Newman got a can of Lite beer from the cooler and drank it as he built the fire. Janet came in from the kitchen with the steaks on a platter. "I put some beans on to heat," she said. She put the steaks down beside Newman. There were tongs on the platter with the steaks. "I'd set the table," Janet said, "but I don't know where to eat. I wouldn't dare disturb Chris's table layout there. He's got everything laid out like he's ready for surgery." She got a bottle of wine from the cooler and poured some into a transparent plastic cup.

Newman said, "We'll eat off our laps, I think. Chris is fairly intense about his set-up."

"But he's right, Aaron. It can't hurt to be ready."

"Yeah, I know. At home we laughed at him lurking around in the yard at night, and goddamned if he didn't save our lives. This is probably sensible. But don't you feel like a horse's ass with the gunbelt and all?"

"Yes, but I'd be a lot more scared without it."

"True."

The fire began to bite into the logs. Janet turned the lights off, and they sat on the floor in front of the fire as the flames began to get bigger and the shadows moved in the room. Newman got another beer.

"Like a vacation," Newman said.

"Or a honeymoon," Janet said.

"Except we came to kill a man," Newman said.

"There's no other way, Aaron."

The smell of the beans cooking on the stovetop mingled with the woodsmoke. Newman drank some beer. "No, there isn't. I'm glad you're here," he said.

"I belong here," she said. "It is our problem. It happened to us."

"I wish it hadn't."

"But it did."

"I wish I could handle it alone."

"But you can't. Who could?"

"I wish I were someone who could. Chris could."

"I wonder," Janet said. "I wonder if he doesn't need an audience to see how good he is. I wonder if he doesn't need a cause to serve, or a crowd to please."

Newman shrugged. "There's guys that could."

"And there's guys that couldn't do this," Janet said. "Guys that would just fold up and do what they were told. You can't be perfect, Aaron."

"I'd like to be better at this."

"You are being the best you can be. You've been a good father and a good husband and a good writer for a long time now. You've always handled everything you had to. You're handling this. Don't muck it up by wanting to be something else. I wouldn't trade you for Chris."

Newman was silent, sitting close to her, not touching. *Chris is none of those things,* he thought looking at the fire. *Chris was a lousy husband and a bad father. He never was able to handle it when the kids were sick or the money was short or the plumbing broke. All he could do was fight. All he's good at is violence.*

"When the going got tough, Chris bailed out," Newman said.

"What?"

"When it got tough at home. When it wasn't fun having kids or wife, Chris would go to the health club or the bars or the gym or hunting. He was tough in fighting, but he wasn't tough in hanging in there."

Janet looked at him. "God, Aaron. I think you're maturing," she said.

"Well it's true," he said, "there's more than one kind of toughness."

She nodded, smiling slightly.

"The thing is, we're in something here that requires a particular kind. I don't know if I've got it."

"I do," Janet said. "I've got it."

22

There were five of them in the boat as they rowed across to the island with the mist still lingering lightly over the lake and the sun slanting very sharply in from the east. Adolph Karl sat in the stern wearing a plaid shirt and new green polyester pants. Beside him, his son Richie, twenty-eight. His son Marty, twenty-six, sat in the bow seat with Frank Marriott. Gordy Tate rowed.

"It's them," Janet said, looking through the binoculars. "Two of them are the ones that tied me up." She handed the glasses to Newman. He looked.

"That's Karl in the stern," he said. "In the plaid shirt."

The Springfield was lying across a shooting rest that Hood had built in the fork of a small white oak at the lake edge, thirty yards from their cabin. Hood adjusted the scope.

"Goddamn," he said.

"What?" Newman was whispering, although the boat was a quarter of a mile away.

"Karl's on the wrong side. The guy with the yellow jacket on is between me and him."

"Shoot both of them," Janet said.

"Let me see," Newman said. His throat was very tight and he had trouble getting his voice out. The boat was halfway across. Hood stepped aside and Newman peered through the scope. There was no fixed sight on the barrel, and the scope was like looking through a telescope. It was as if there were no gun. He could see part of Karl's checkered shirt and the back of his head. More and less of him came into view as both he and Richie moved as they talked and Tate rowed.

"We could hit him," Newman whispered. "There will never be another chance as good. We could hit him and get in the car and be on the road and they wouldn't even know where the shot came from. By the time they rowed to shore we'd be gone."

"Let me see," Hood said. Newman stepped aside.

"We can do it," Newman said.

"Do it, Chris," Janet said. "Do it now."

Hood stared through the scope.

"For crissake, Chris, shoot," Newman said.

Hood held the rifle carefully in its shooting rest, his cheek against the stock, his hand curled around the curved pistol grip line of the stock, his forefinger on the trigger. His left arm was almost fully extended, steadying the rifle in its rest. He inhaled once, let out the air, and then was perfectly still.

Newman said silently, *Shoot, shoot, shoot, shoot.* Somewhere on the lake a fish broke. Hood inhaled, and relaxed his grip on the rifle. He straightened.

"No good," he said. "Too risky. We'll have to try for a better shot."

Newman felt his eyes fill with tears. "Jesus Christ," he said.

Janet Newman pushed past Hood and crouched over the rifle. She looked through the sight. Newman could see the rowboat disappear behind the dock. Janet stood up. She didn't say anything. She walked back toward the house. Newman followed her. Hood picked up the binoculars and began to study Karl's island.

In the house Newman smashed his hand down on the table where the packs and weapons were laid out. The rifles jounced. "Fuck," he said. His voice was shaking. "We could have done it and been gone. It could have been over now. Son of a bitch." He hit the table again.

"There's nothing to be done," Janet Newman said. "We'll have to wait for the next chance, but this time you or I will have to do it. We'll have to stop waiting for Chris to do it. We'll shoot as soon as we can."

The rowboat went back and forth two more times that day, but Karl wasn't in it. It went to and from the island three times the next day, without Karl. The third time it returned to the island it was powered by an outboard motor. The next morning a second boat with an outboard went out to the island. And at eight-five that morning both boats pulled away from the dock, went around the far side of the island, and headed down the lake.

Hood came in from his post at the rifle stand, hurrying.

"Grab the packs," he said, "they're running."

Newman and Janet each picked up a pack by the straps, and a long gun, and followed Hood out of the cabin and down toward the canoe. On the lake, a quarter of a mile away, the two rowboats moved slowly east, driven by the small outboard engines.

Janet Newman sat on the floor in the middle of the canoe. Newman took the bow paddle, Hood the stern. The canoe moved out from the dock and turned east after the two rowboats. It was eight-thirty in the morning, the sun was up and shining in their eyes, skipping brightly off the water of the lake. There was no wind. The canoe went around a small point and the dock was out of sight. White oak and red maple pushed down close to the water; many had fallen in where the banks had eroded and given way. There was nothing alive in sight except the two rowboats ahead of them in the sun.

"We'll stay close to the shore," Hood said, "like we're just canoeing."

"Can we stay with them, paddling?" Janet said.

"Yeah," Hood said. "The outboards are only little ones. They're not going to leave us."

"Lake's not that big," Newman said.

"But there's an outlet," Hood said. "According to my map the ponds connect and there's access to the Saco River."

"So we could be in for a long trip," Janet said.

"If we have to trail them for long they'll get suspicious," Newman said.

Hood didn't say anything. The canoe moved easily in the water. Behind them something broke in the water. They could hear the splash. A loon dived between them and the outboards. The sun moved higher. Newman could feel the sweat begin to break on his forehead and the muscles starting to loosen. Hood guided the canoe easily. Newman was a strong paddle in the bow.

"Chris," Newman said. "What the hell did you mean, 'they're running'?"

"They're moving out," Hood said.

"But they aren't running from us, specifically. That is, there's nothing as far as they know chasing them."

"No. They weren't hurrying. They weren't running. It was just an expression."

A painted turtle slipped off a semisubmerged log and hung motionless in the water, only its head exposed as the canoe passed. Hood guided the canoe out farther from the lake shore. In close the shore was thick with the snags of fallen timber. There were slick black branches just below the surface.

The packs and the long guns were on the floor of the canoe.

"We're going to run out of lake pretty soon," Newman said. The lake water was the color of strong tea. Looking down Newman could see swarms of fry moving below the eddy of his paddle. Janet Newman had the field glasses on the two rowboats. "They're turning," she said.

The two boats moved slowly in an arc to the left and moved at right angles to the east end of the lake shore.

"We'll keep paddling along the shoreline," Hood said. "If they keep going around the edge of the lake like that we can see them and we can cut across and catch up if we have to. This way it doesn't look like we're following them and we're still keeping them in sight." Hood wore a gray woolen shirt with the sleeves rolled up past the elbows, denim pants, and hiking boots. Newman had on a blue woolen shirt with the sleeves rolled, cream-colored corduroy pants, and hiking boots. They continued to paddle along the shoreline, slowly curving north.

The sun was almost straight overhead when Janet

said, "They're landing." Hood and Newman let the
canoe drift as they looked back and across the lake.
The two boats were near shore, and they could make
out one of the men wading ashore.

"The great big one has gotten out," Janet said,
watching through the binoculars. "He's pulling both
boats up onto a little beach."

As they drifted, the canoe paddles laid across the
gunnels of the canoe, they watched the two rowboats
across the lake empty. There were the same five people. Karl, his two sons, and Tate and Marriott.

"They each have a pack," Janet said. "And rifles.
The packs are a lot larger than ours. They have, what
are they called, packboards."

The five men walked away from the boats and into
the woods.

"What now?" Newman said.

"We'll follow them," Hood said. "Let's paddle."

Both men dug the paddle blades hard into the water, turning their bodies, bending their backs. The
canoe slid forward. As they paddled they fell into
rhythm with each other, their bodies bending steadily
and together, the paddles digging into the dark water.
Newman felt the sweat running along his back. Cutting across the foot of the lake they were a hundred
yards down-lake of the rowboats in half an hour.

"We'll go in here," Hood said, and turned the canoe
into a cove. A single mink frog plopped off a stone
into the water. Hood guided the canoe between two
large rocks. Newman reached out and balanced the
canoe with a hand on each rock and stepped out. He
was in calf-deep water. He pulled the canoe through
so that its forward third rested on the bank. Janet
handed his rifle and pack to him, picked up her own

and, carefully balancing in the half-steady canoe, came out after him and stepped ashore. Hood followed.

"Secure the canoe," he said. He leaned the Springfield against a tree and moved off into the woods at a silent trot; as he went he took out the .45 and thumbed back the hammer. Newman leaned his Winchester beside the Springfield. He took Janet's carbine and put it against the same rock. Then he and Janet pulled the canoe up onto the small beach of pebbles and coarse sand at the foot of the cut bank. Newman tied the bow to a black birch sapling with the mooring line.

Then each of them slipped on their knapsacks and waited, listening. There were birds. They must have been in the woods all the time, but in the tense silence as they listened for danger Newman heard them as he had not before. He saw every flutter among the trees as possible danger, and his senses sharpened to them. He picked up the Winchester. Janet held the carbine.

"Pull the bolt," he said.

It snicked loudly in the thick green shadows. Thick stands of white pine mingled with the oak and maple. He worked the lever on the Winchester. The sound was loud and metallic.

"Christ, you can hear that in Quebec," Newman said. He was whispering.

The birds moved in the trees, darting, fluttering, their voices in various pitches and speeds. He saw bluejays and once a grosbeak with a faint rosy blush on its breast. He heard what he thought from childhood memory was a catbird. The lake made motion noise as it eddied slightly against the small grainy beach.

A red-winged blackbird flashed across the brief

opening between two trees. Newman jumped very slightly. Then he heard the sound of something larger moving through the woods. It was to his right. He turned, bringing the rifle up as something moved in the bushes. As he aimed he moved his body between Janet and the movement. He didn't know he was doing it. The movement clarified and Chris Hood came out of the woods. Newman exhaled and put his hand behind him and touched Janet.

Shit, he thought. *I'm shielding her.* He felt brave. *I did it involuntarily. My instincts are good.*

"They've moved out," Hood said. "There's a trail leads up from where they beached the boats, and they've followed it. Come on."

They followed him to the place where the boats were beached, empty, the motors tilted up.

"Do you know where they're going?" Janet said.

"Deeper into the woods," Hood said. "Look." He brought out a detailed map of the area. "I picked this up at the sporting goods store in town. We're about here, I figure. We were going east into the sunrise all morning and then we turned here, and I figure this is the cove we passed back there."

Newman looked at the map. "There's nothing but woods forever," he said.

"Then we have them this time," Janet said.

Newman looked up from the map.

Hood said, "Yes."

Newman said, "You've got five armed men trapped in a thousand miles of woods. I'm not sure we've got them cornered."

"Help me with the boats," Hood said. He overturned one of them and with his hatchet chopped a hole in the bottom. "Do the other one," he said.

"If they didn't know something was up," Newman said, "they will when they get back here."

"They'll head back here if we don't get them first, and when they get here we'll have them trapped against the lake." Hood was excited. His movements were quick. Newman turned the second boat over and sank the hatchet blade into the plywood bottom. He chopped a hole several inches around in the bottom, prying the splintering plywood with the hatchet blade.

"Better hide the canoe," he said.

"Yes," Hood said. "I'll take it down-lake a little ways and hide it and come back up here. You and Janet wait here and watch. You better get out of sight."

They helped him push the canoe back off the beach, and they watched him paddle from the stern, turning the paddle blade after each stroke to hold the canoe steady. When he went around the near curve of the lake, Newman turned and looked for a place to hide.

"Under the big pine tree," he said to Janet, "behind those rocks. I hope they don't come back while Chris is gone."

"Me too," Janet said. They slipped under the tree and lay on their stomachs behind the gray rocks.

"You too?" Newman said. "You sound scared."

"I am."

"I thought you weren't," he said.

"I wasn't. But I am now."

"How come?"

"It's the woods, I think. It's so alien."

"Or we are," he said.

The rocks behind which they lay were gray, granite flecked with quartz. Grayish lichen grew over parts of them. The dead pine-needles had made a thick, soft blanket around the base of the tree and no vegetation had been able to push up through it.

"Aaron, destoying those boats has really committed us."

"I know."

"If they come back they'll know."

"They'll know something," Newman said. "But they won't necessarily know what."

"But they'll be very much more wary, and there are five to our three."

"Right. It's better if we surprise them before they see the boats."

There was a locust keen in the air, and the noise of a woodpecker.

"You seem better, Aaron."

"How so?"

"Less—what?—ambivalent, I guess. Less tied in a knot, more ready, looser."

"If rape is inevitable, lay back and enjoy it," Newman said.

"Meaning?"

"Meaning I'm committed. It's too late to agonize. I'm scared, but I'm not uncertain, you know."

"I guess so."

"You're kind of nice yourself," he said.

"Like what?"

"Like not so bossy, not so controlling. Softer, maybe."

"I just react to you," she said. "If you don't push at me, I don't have to push back."

Newman made a harsh, derisive sound. "Family that kills together stays together," he said.

There was movement along the lake and Chris Hood appeared, walking quietly.

Janet said, "Over here, Chris."

Hood slid under the tree with them. "Canoe's in the cover just around the point," he said. "I put some rocks in it and sank it in about three feet of water. It's under the water at the base of the only big rocks in the cove."

Newman nodded.

"Remember where it is," Hood said. "In case I don't come back with you."

"Maybe none of us will come back," Newman said.

"Then it won't matter," Hood said.

23

The trail was little more than a continuous opening in the thick forest. It was laced with greenbrier and slow going. But all around them the greenbrier was thicker, and brush and second-growth saplings were dense and difficult.

Occasionally there were the soft summer droppings of whitetail deer. "In winter," Hood said softly, "the droppings are much more like pellets because the feed is different. In the winter they're eating bark, stuff like that."

Hood was first as they went single file, the Springfield cradled across his left arm, his right hanging free. Janet came next and Newman was third. They smelled of insect repellent and perspiration. But Newman wasn't tired.

"I'm not that taken up with deer shit, Chris," Newman said in a loud whisper.

Hood smiled. "You're in the woods, Aaron, its good to know a little about them."

It was late afternoon. The sun was still high but the deep woods were dim. They had been walking for three and a half hours.

"You okay, Janet?" Hood said.

"I'm fine," she said.

Newman smiled to himself. "She's in shape, Chris. She runs three miles a day."

Hood nodded. Janet looked back at Newman. He winked at her and made the double-time gesture with his clenched fist. Ahead there were gunshots. Hood stopped, raised his right hand. They stood motionless.

"Deer maybe," Newman said.

"Out of season," Hood said.

"Christ, so am I," Newman said. "That didn't seem to sweat them."

"Yeah, maybe. I guess they wouldn't be nervous about the game laws, would they?"

They were quiet. No more shots. No sounds. No locust hum. No birdsong. Newman could hear Janet breathing in front of him. Her shirt below the pack was soaked with sweat, and he could smell the perspiration odor mingled with perfume and insect repellent. He liked it.

A woodpecker began to drum in the darkening trees above them. There was locust hum again. Hood motioned with his hand and they went forward behind him walking with very little noise. The forest was deep with the accumulated leaf-fall of timeless autumns, and the footing was soft. They walked carefully, watching where they walked, not stepping on dead branches.

It must have been like this, Newman thought, *when the Saint Francis Indians would raid down into Maine and take prisoners back up to Canada and Rogers' Rangers would chase them.* In his imagination he could sense the single file of coppery men and the long-dressed women captives with mop hats on moving in silence, the women stumbling sometimes, and behind them the lank men in fringed buckskins and loose-sleeved shirts moving grimly at the trot, carrying long rifles. *Like us*, Newman thought, *in pursuit.*

The trail opened slightly by a small stream. Newman could smell faintly the acrid edge of gunpowder, a dim nasal memory of Korea. At the stream edge was the buff-colored short body of a groundhog. Where its head had been was a scramble of blood, bone, and tissue. They stopped. They spoke softly.

"Shot it with a big gun," Hood said.

"No season on these things," Newman said. "Guess you can shoot them anytime."

"Not a lot of sport to it," Hood said.

"Why shoot a groundhog?" Janet said.

"Cause it was there," Newman said.

"They're not choosy," Hood said. "Remember that."

They went on. It was nearly dark now and they went more slowly, Hood ahead, listening hard, watching closely, slowing at each trail turn. For the last hour the trail had meandered, rising slowly. Newman could feel the rise and the added stress of it. He watched Janet carefully. She did not seem more tired that he was. They'd canoed and walked all day without eating. He was hungry. It wasn't an insistent hunger, he was too intent on the pursuit and the trail ahead of them to be preoccupied with hunger, but the knowledge that he'd like to eat was always a part of his consciousness.

In front of them, Hood stopped and put his hand up. He made an exaggerated sniffing gesture with his head. Newman smelled smoke. Hood looked at him; Newman nodded. They could barely see each other now that the evening had gathered. Hood came back and stood close to Janet and Newman.

"I'd guess they're making camp for the night," he said.

"What do we do?" Janet said.

"We'll find a place to squat and then reconnoiter. If they are making camp we ought to be able to do what we came for tonight and walk out of here."

"With the rest of them chasing us," Newman said.

"Kill them all," Hood said.

"No," Newman said. "Five people, Jesus Christ."

"Aaron, this is like a war," Janet said.

Newman shook his head. "I'll murder Karl," he said. "Because we have to, because it's right and necessary. But I won't ambush and kill five sleeping men. I can't."

"Aaron," Janet began.

Hood said, "Shhh. First we find a place to locate. Then we'll work out a plan." He moved off the trail into the thickets. It was impossible to be silent, but they moved quietly. It was fully dark now and they held hands as they moved off the trail. Newman held the Winchester upright before his face as a shield against the branches he could no longer see. He heard Janet yip with pain in front of him.

"Put the gun straight up and down in front of your nose," he whispered. "Keep the branches from hitting you in the eye." She did as he told her.

They found some space where a granite outcropping rose eight feet above them. Newman could see the stars, and in their light he could see around him a short way. They took the packs off and put them down.

"I'm going to eat a granola bar," Newman said.

"Just one," Hood said. "We don't know how long we'll be."

Newman nodded and bit into the bar.

Hood said, "Janet, you stick here with the packs; Aaron and I will sneak over for a look, and then when we know what the situation is we'll come back and talk it out."

"I'll come with you," she said.

"There's no need," Hood said. "And someone has to watch the packs."

"I'm going to come," Janet said. "If you get lost or have to run or something I won't be stuck here alone. Wear the packs."

"She's right, Chris. She should come. Besides, we might need her gun."

"A woman doesn't belong on patrol, Aaron." Hood was looking at the ground.

Newman didn't say anything. He looked at Janet. She opened her mouth. Closed it. Opened it again, breathed in quickly and out quickly and said, "For my protection, Chris. I need you to get me out of here. I'm afraid to be alone."

Hood still looked at the ground. He nodded three times. "Yeah. Okay, I guess you do. Remember we came uphill to get here. If we get separated, the lake is downhill. Facing uphill the trail is to our left now. Listen to my signal." Hood whistled through his teeth, the first syllable long, the second rounder: *see soo*. He repeated it. "It's a kind of night-hawk sound. If there's a woodsman among them. When I make it that's the time to come back here; if we get separated I'll make it periodically. You try."

Newman whistled *see soo*. Janet whistled.

Hood shook his head. "Sounds too human. Whistle through your teeth."

Newman said, "It rhymes with 'see through,' like in 'see-through blouse.'"

Janet whistled again. *See soo.*

"Good."

They moved back toward the smell of smoke. Very slowly, side by side now, not single file. They slipped past the clumps of sumac, among the saplings, their feet catching in greenbrier and Virginia creeper, and occasionally wild blackberry and raspberry bushes. Sweat and time had wiped away the insect repellent and the bugs were thick and merciless in the dense woods. Newman stayed beside Janet. Hood was to their right. They couldn't see him.

Ahead of him through the trees Newman could see the moving light of a fire. The smell of smoke was strong, and the smell of cured meat cooking had mixed with the woodsmoke. He could hear the slightly artificial sound of a radio playing. He edged slowly closer. The radio sound was a ballgame. Karl and his party had camped in an open area by a small stream that ran over a nearly flat rock the size of a pool table and dropped into a narrow bed below the rock, where it trickled down the long slope toward the lake. It was a natural campsite and the ground was smooth and clear around the tiny waterfall, as if worn smooth by campers since before Columbus.

An igloo-shaped round orange tent had been set up, a fire was burning in a circle of stones on the bare ground in the middle of the clearing. Adolph Karl sat on the ground, leaning against a packboard and drinking from a large leather-covered flask. His son Richie sat on his haunches by the fire, cooking sausages in a fry pan set on a small wire rack over the flames. Frank Marriott and Marty Karl were playing cards on a blanket spread before the tent. Marty took the flask from his father and drank. He passed it on to Marriott.

Newman made a slight downward pressure on Janet's arm with his right hand. He held the Winchester in his left. She dropped to the ground and lay flat watching the camp. Newman remained standing for another moment, looking at the camp. *The tent would be for Karl,* he thought. *He'll sleep in it and the rest of them will sleep outside. It's only big enough for him and maybe one other. If he sleeps there alone it's a chance to get him and slip away. But not with a gun . . . with a knife? Could I do it with a knife? Maybe Chris can. He did it before. Maybe Janet. Maybe I can.*

He heard something move in the brush. He half-turned and a heavy object exploded against the side of his face. He stumbled backward. He wanted to use the Winchester but he couldn't find it. It wasn't in his hand. He was closer to the fire, and then he was very close to it. He closed his eyes for a moment and opened them and looked at the mottled tan of a puff-ball almost in his eye. He smelled dirt. He was on the ground.

A voice said, "I was taking a leak when I spotted him prowling around with a gun, Dolph."

The voice was familiar.

"Here's the gun," it said.

Another voice said, "Get him on his feet and look through his pockets. See who he is." Newman didn't know the voice. But he knew the first one. He was trying to remember where he knew it from when he felt himself jerked upright. He swayed slightly as he stood. Someone's hand held the back of his shirt collar. Someone unbuckled the pistol belt. He smelled body sweat and bad breath and whiskey. His vision was fuzzy, but he could see. Adolph Karl and he remembered. He felt his stomach shrink in upon itself. He half-turned as a hand took his wallet. He saw the huge man and he remembered more. He remembered the voice. The huge man had hold of the back of his shirt collar, holding him up easily with his left hand. With his right he tossed the wallet to Karl. The huge man looked at Newman as Newman looked, twisting half around, at him.

"Motherfucker," the huge man said. "I know this guy. He's one of the guys I saw in the alley."

Karl looked at Newman without expression. Richie Karl pointed a shotgun at Newman. Karl took Newman's driver's license out of the wallet and looked at it. He looked at Newman and back at the license. He turned it so he could see the picture better. Then he put the license back in the wallet and tossed the wallet into the fire.

He looked at Newman again. "He's the guy that fingered me," Karl said. "The fucking asshole."

24

"What are you doing here?" Karl said.

Newman was motionless. He fought against the impulse to look for Chris and Janet. They must be out there. Janet had seen it. She'd been right beside him on the ground. Chris. Did Chris know? He was separate from Janet. What if he'd started back? What if Janet couldn't rescue him?

The huge man had transferred his grip to Newman's upper arms, one hand on each.

"What are you doing here?" Karl said. There was no tone in his voice. It sounded mechanical.

Newman stayed still. His face hurt. His head ached. His stomach felt bottomless. He was nearly dizzy with fear.

"Marty," Karl said. "Stick his face in the fire till he answers me."

Karl's younger son stepped toward Newman. He was as tall as his father, and fleshy, with an insufficient moustache over a Cupid's-bow mouth. He wore a black sweat shirt on which was printed "The Helmet Law Sucks." He put his right hand behind Newman's neck and began to bend him forward. Newman stiffened his neck and swelled the big trapezius muscles he had earned through years of weight training. Marty couldn't bend him, but the huge man could. He pressed forward and down on Newman's arms, forcing Newman toward the ground, forcing the knees to bend. *It's humiliating. Torture isn't just pain, it's public humiliation.* He strained against the pressure of Marty's hand and the huge man's force. He was losing. *Where the fuck are they?* His knees touched, he could feel the fire.

Chris Hood stepped out from behind the orange pup tent and hit the huge man across the back of the head with the butt of the Springfield. The huge man let go of Newman and pitched sideways and sat down. Without the pressure of the huge man Newman uncoiled like a released spring.

He straightened, tearing loose from Marty's grasp. He pushed Marty away from him and jumped for the woods. Richie Karl brought the shotgun up and from the shelter of the trees Janet Newman shot him five times. Hood turned the Springfield at Karl and Frank Marriott shot him in the chest with a .357 magnum. Hood died at once.

Newman turned toward the sounds of Janet's shots and she caught his hand as he reached the dark shelter of the forest. He went ahead of her, she followed, holding on to his hand in the darkness as they blundered as fast as they could through the woods. As they ran, Newman had a vague sense of downhill. He bore left in the darkness, feeling the panic boil in him and fighting to keep it down. They came across some granite outcroppings and stopped.

"Is this the place we were?" Newman's breath was coming in gasps. The sweat ran off his face.

"I don't know," Janet said. She was panting.

"Shh."

They listened. There was no sound of pursuit. He tried to keep his breathing silent so he could listen. The woods were empty of human sound except his own.

"Where's Chris?" Newman said. His breathing was still harsh and labored.

"I think they shot him," Janet said.

"Jesus Christ," Newman said. "Are you sure?"

"I saw him fall," Janet said, "then we ran. I don't know. I think so."

"Oh, good Jesus," Newman said. "We're on our own."

Janet nodded.

"Jesus, Jesus," Newman said.

"We can do it," Janet said.

"What if he's not dead," Newman said, "and they've got him?"

Janet was silent.

"We'll have to help him," Newman said.

"If he's not dead."

"We have to know," Newman said. "Jesus, what a mess."

"Nothing's changed," Janet said. "There's one fewer of us and at least one fewer of them. The odds are still the same."

"Except they know we're here." Newman's breathing was easier. He looked at his wife in the dim light where the stars shone into the clearing. "You shot the one with the shotgun."

"Yes."

"Just like I showed you."

"Breathe, Aim, Slack, Squeeze," she said.

"He would have killed me."

"That's why I shot him."

"How do you feel?"

"Scared, out of wind, mad. Like you," she said.

"But you killed a guy. You've never done that before. Does it bother you?"

"No. It had to be done. I don't mind. I won't mind next time either."

"You are a tough cookie," Newman said. "Thank God."

"No, I don't think that's it, Aaron. It might be hard if it were right close and you had to wrestle and gouge or if you knew the person. But at fifty feet with someone I don't know it's easy. Squeeze the trigger. Just like you put the brakes on in a car. Something happens, you react. Didn't you ever kill anyone in Korea?"

"I don't think so. I was a radio operator at battalion level. I heard shots fired in anger, but I didn't kill anyone I can recall."

"Well, we'll have to kill several now. And you'll have to do some of it."

"I know," Newman said. "They know who we are. They'll figure out what we were doing here. If they get out of here alive we're dead."

"And the girls," Janet said, "they may well be dead too."

Newman grunted as if he'd been hit.

"So," Janet said, "let's get organized."

Newman sat behind the outcropping of granite in the woods in the dark and rubbed his temples with his left hand. As he sat the sweat cooled on his body and he felt cold.

"It's September," he said.

"What?"

"Cold," Newman said, "it gets cold up here in September."

"Yes."

"They took my rifle, and pistol belt."

"Take the carbine and my ax," Janet said.

"Yes, and you have the .32 and the knife. We have the jackets and the down vests. I have eleven granola bars. You?"

"Twelve."

"We ought to try and get by on one a day and stretch them out. Try to live off the land as much as we can."

"Yes."

"We'll eat one each morning. Then we'll look for berries and stuff. If we've found nothing by night we'll have another one."

"I hope we're not here that long."

"Even if we can get them, and they don't get us, we may get lost. Neither one of us is big in the woods."

"You won't get lost," Janet said. "You've never been lost in your life."

"I've never spent time in the woods."

"I'll bet they haven't either," Janet said.

"I hope not."

25

They slept very little that night, though they tried, huddled together, each in a thigh-length nylon pullover.

"You try and sleep and I'll watch," Newman had said. "Then I'll wake you when I'm falling asleep and you watch."

But in fact neither one of them slept, and after an hour and a half they realized they weren't going to and they sat quiet in the dark and listened to the twittering of insects and waited for the morning. It came, finally, with a slow thinning of the darkness. The sky behind the treetops got paler. Then the trees and rocks around them began to take shape. They could begin to see where they were and what it looked like.

"We've got to sneak back to the camp and see," Newman said.

"Yes."

"You look pretty good for a broad who slept on the ground in her clothes."

"What I wonder is if they're sneaking about, looking for us," Janet said.

All business, he thought, *even here. Getting in charge.*

"Take the carbine," she said.

"Okay."

The sun began to rise. Newman looked at it carefully, turning his body so the sun was to his right. In his mental map he saw himself standing on the East Coast, near the Atlantic, looking at Canada, full-sized, like someone in a television commercial.

"Okay," he said, "uphill is essentially north, downhill is essentially south. To get back to the lake we want to go south, downhill, remember that. In case we're separated."

"How about the packs?" Janet said.

"We'll bring them."

"Easier to be sneaking around without them."

"But if we leave them someplace we may not find them again and we need them," Newman said. "We better bring them."

She nodded and slipped into hers. It pleased him that she did what he said without argument. *Not because I said so, though, because she agreed.*

"Let's go," she said.

He picked up the carbine. "I'm not even sure which way," he said. "I'd say northwest."

"Which way is that?" she said.

He'd known she wouldn't know. "Bear left, uphill," he said. "Remember, uphill is north. When you face north, west is to your left."

"Why not say left and right then?"

"Because left and right are relative to the way you're standing but north and south are not."

She was impatient. "Let's go," she said.

"All right, but let me go first," he said. "You tend to get lost."

She nodded and they moved out of the small clearing. *It feels like I'm leaving a refuge,* he thought. *It's no safer here than anywhere else but because we spent about eight hours here it's familiar and it feels safer. Amazing how we adjust. Safety may turn out to be relative too.*

It was full daylight. He moved very slowly through the woods ahead of her. Walking very carefully, putting each foot down thoughtfully, feeling his way through the ground bramble and princess pine that tangled underfoot. He stopped frequently to listen. The second time he stopped there was a thicket of black raspberries. He gestured at them. And they both picked and ate as many as were ripe.

"Blackberries?" she said softly.

"Black raspberries I think. The blackberry bushes are taller and these don't have that oblong blackberry look, you know."

"How the hell do you know how high black raspberry bushes are?" she said.

He shrugged. "I read it somewhere."

"I'm finished," she said.

He nodded and they moved on, bearing slightly west and slightly uphill, listening. Stopping, moving very slowly a careful step at a time. He held the carbine in his right hand. His finger on the trigger guard but not on the trigger, the barrel pointing down. It was a light weapon; with the fifteen-round clip fully loaded it weighed just over six pounds and it fitted comfortably in one hand. He could even fire it with one hand should he need to.

The forest was handsome. There were white and

gray birch, white pine, and oak. There were clumps of
second-growth saplings and the low tangle of ground
vines. The ascending sun made shade and light pat-
terns through the tree leaves. Even though it was only
early September, the sumac this far north was beginning to show color. He couldn't see very far, and as he
moved through the woods he looked and listened with
physical effort, feeling the stress of his concentration
tightening the muscles of his neck and shoulders.

As the day warmed the insects became more active
and Newman stopped to put insect repellent on himself and his wife. Their hum was still frustrating but
they didn't bite. Birds moved and sang in the trees
and before them in the bushes. There were squirrels,
too, looking to Newman oddly out of place in the
woods, as if they belonged in parks and front yards.
Christ, Newman thought, *pretty soon I'll run into
some pigeons and then I'll see a wino sleeping on a
bench.*

They had walked in silence and tension for an hour
when they cut the trail. Here, where they crossed it,
the trail was rutted slightly, and worn in some places to
bare earth. He raised his right hand, palm open. Janet
stopped behind him, next to his shoulder.

"Is it the same trail?" she whispered.

"Must be," he whispered. "How many can there be
up here?"

"Which way is their camp?"

"I'm not sure," he said. "I can't tell if we are above it
or below it. I'd guess we're below it. If we were above
it I'd assume we would have crossed that stream."

"Are you sure?"

"No, but it stands to reason. The stream was running southwest. We've been moving northwest. If we

were above their campsite we should have crossed the stream."

"I still don't see why."

"Well, take my word on it," he said. "If you can't picture it, I don't have time to draw a picture for you."

She was silent.

"Of course streams will go strange ways, they follow the land." He was talking so she could hear, but in fact he was talking to himself. He often did that, talked to her so he could hear himself think. "But all we can do is go with the best guess, the most reasonable possibility."

He pointed up the trail with his forefinger, making a decisive stabbing motion with his hand, his thumb cocked.

She said, "I still don't see . . ." and stopped talking as he looked at her.

She nodded. They stood together looking up the trail.

"We can't just walk up to it," she said.

"I know. We'll have to go along it in the woods. Every little while we'll swing over and cross the trail. Then we'll go a ways and swing back over and so on. That way we make sure that the trail's still there."

"What do you think they're doing?" she said.

"If it were me I'd hide in the woods near camp and wait for us to come back. But I don't know. They're used to bullying people and having people scared of them. They may think we're running. They may be crazy mad. They may chase us."

"So you think they are out in the woods trying to find us?"

"Either way," he said. "Maybe in ambush. Maybe chasing us."

"Well don't we have to know which?" she said.

"We can't," he said.

"But can't you make a guess?"

"No. We have to assume both things. Sort of a variation of negative capability."

"I don't like it," she said.

"Me either," he said, "but there it is."

"Well, let's go. The sooner we find them the sooner this is over with."

They began to move up the trail, keeping to the right of it fifty feet, looking and listening carefully. There was wind, more than had blown since they went into the wilderness. It was not uncomfortable, but it stirred the branches as if someone were there, and it rustled the leaves as if someone were coming. They moved even more slowly and carefully. Hearing the bird and insect noises, the tree noises, the sound of their own movement.

The noise of the woods was continuous. It was one of the things that surprised him most about the forest. It was never quiet. The great, still forest of his imagination was derived from photographs and paintings. The real forest was always alive. Birds, frogs, cicada, squirrels, and things he didn't know of chirped and chittered and keened and hummed and grunted and rustled day and night. He was listening for human sounds.

It took them an hour to go a mile. Newman had a red scratch starting at the corner of his left eye and running across his cheek, and Janet's lip was puffy from an insect bite. Newman's stomach rolled emptily as if it had overreacted to the handful of raspberries it had gotten and was now digesting more than it had received.

They turned left and crossed the trail. It had veered toward them and they were barely ten feet from it.

"Jesus," Newman said, "not good. We might have walked right into them. We're too close."

They crossed the trail and stopped forty-five feet into the woods on the left side of it. "We shouldn't be walking bunched together like this," he said. "If we blunder into them they could kill us both with one shot."

"I'm not going to walk alone," she said. "I'll get lost."

He looked back behind him. "Stay behind me as far as you can and still keep me in sight. Then if I'm nabbed you can still operate. You saved me last time."

"All right, but if I whistle like Chris taught us"—she whistled softly between her teeth, *see soo*—"you wait and if you don't see me, come back."

He nodded. "If you get lost stay where you are. I'll find you. Otherwise we'll go around in circles for each other."

She turned away to look back of them. "Of course they could come up behind us."

"Yes," he said. "You're no safer back there. We cover each other. If I need you I'll whistle the same way." He smiled at her. "You know how to whistle don't you?"

"Just pucker up and blow," she said. She smiled. It was an old joke from a favorite movie. And it seemed somehow to ease the oddness of their situation.

26

They found Karl's camp in the early afternoon. Newman saw the orange tent through the trees. He raised his hand. Twenty feet behind him Janet stopped. Her hair was wet with sweat and stuck close to her head. There were scratches on her face. Newman gestured her forward and she came up beside him. She had the .32 in her hand. Newman put one finger to his lips. Then he pointed at the tent. She nodded. He could feel the vertigo in his stomach. His legs felt weak. He looked at her face, scratched and sweaty, without makeup, showing strong bone structure and no fear. He'd looked at the face so long it seemed somehow permanent. He felt reassured, safer with her beside him.

They listened. There was no human sound from the camp. He put his lips close to her ear.

"We'll circle it," he said. "If they are staking it out we'll come behind them."

She nodded.

"Remember," he whispered, "you only have five shots in that thing before you have to reload. Don't waste them."

She nodded again. They started very carefully around the camp. A quarter of the way around the camp's perimeter they found Hood's body. It was thirty yards from where he had died. It lay facedown under some low-clumped sumac. One hand was under him and the other lay palm up by his side. The fingers half closed. Ants crawled in the cup of the hand and more ants crawled around the black area of dried blood between his shoulder blades where the bullets had emerged. Death had released Hood's sphincter control. Janet put her clenched fist against her mouth. Newman looked down once, and looked away. He put one hand on Janet's arm and moved her away from Hood's body.

It took them ninety-six minutes to complete the circle. No one was near the camp.

"Let's get closer," Newman said.

Crouched, they inched closer to the clearing and stopped finally, squatting beneath the down-swooping bows of an old white pine tree, silent on the thick mulch of needles around the foot-thick base of the tree. There was a cluster of stones grouped to form a fireplace, but there was no fire. The orange tent had its flap open. A packboard lay by the open flap. Around the fireplace there were several camp cookery utensils. Starlings were pecking at something in one of the pans. Three sleeping bags, still unrolled, spread out around the fireplace like spokes from a hub. The foil wrappings of freeze-dried food were scattered about the clearing. A half-full bottle of Canadian Club stood on the ground near the tent. Two packboards leaned against the flat rock over which the stream flowed. Another packboard hung from a tree behind the tent. A ground squirrel skittered across the clearing. The sun slanted from the west now, behind them, and dust motes danced in its rays in the silent space. Fresh dirt and a mound of stones at the far edge of the clearing showed where they had buried the boy.

"What now?" she whispered.

He shook his head.

"Let's destroy it," she said.

He looked at her. Faintly, almost like an internal sound, a ruffed grouse drummed far off. The sound registered only at the edge of Newman's mind. "Okay," he said. "Let's do it."

He looked around him. "Get kindling, dry twigs, sticks, leaves, we'll pile them in the tent and then throw everything in there and set it going."

"What about a forest fire?"

He shook his head. "Woods are green. There's been a lot of rain. The tent is surrounded by dirt. Shouldn't spread far."

"Aren't you going to get kindling?" she said.

"No. I want to be able to shoot when we step out there if they really were hiding and we missed them."

She nodded and gathered an armload of dry sticks and twigs. "Okay," she said.

He said, "Stay down. We'll scooch out behind the tent and cut a hole in the back and stuff the brush in that way."

"What if they're back that way?"

"Then we get shot at. But if they're not they won't see us. It cuts down the odds. If we go in the front way they can see us from every place."

"Let's go," she said and handed him her knife.

He went to his knees, the carbine pushing before

him in his right hand, the knife in his left, and crawled into the clearing. Nothing happened. He crawled to the tent. No sound. The starlings continued to forage in the cookware. He drove the point of the knife through the nylon fabric of the tent and sawed a hole. No one was inside. He peered through. There was an open sleeping bag, a roll of toilet paper, a pack, nothing else. He gestured to Janet and she pushed her armload of tinder into the tent. With the hunting knife he whittled some shavings and scraps of bark from one of the sticks. He crumbled several handfuls of the toilet paper. Then he took a butane lighter from his shirt pocket and lit the paper and shavings. The flame caught the paper at once, flickered at the edge of the shavings. A tiny spiral of smoke rose. Then the flame began to nibble into the wood in a tiny black-edged crescent. Newman moved more twigs and bark scraps closer. The fire spread.

"Let's get the other stuff," he said.

They stood up, Newman's eyes scanning the blank wood-line around them, and ran for the packboards. "Take that one on the tree," Newman said.

His wife shoved it into the tent. The flames were crackling now in the dry wood. The sleeping bag began to smolder. Janet ran to the other side of the clearing and picked up another packboard. Her husband had two slung by the shoulder straps over his left arm. He held the knife blade in his teeth and the carbine in his right hand. He threw the two packboards into the tent through the open front flap. Janet put the last packboard in. The sleeping bag was burning.

"Will the tent burn?" Janet said.

"It's nylon," Newman said. "It should melt, and when it does it will carry the burning meltage into the pile of packs and stuff. Or it should."

They turned and slipped back into the shadow of the woods. Behind them the tent fabric began to shrink and then coalesce. Holes appeared in it as burning trickles of melted chemical dropped onto the fire below. The fire burned hotter. "Uphill," Newman said.

She followed him without a sound as they climbed over the tabletop rock and splashed through the stream that splayed across it. Behind them ammunition in the packs began to explode in rattling pops. The tent diminished into a seething wallow of chemicals and flame. The smell of it filled the woods, oddly foreign, an industrial smell in the pristine forest. The starlings flew away.

The upgrade was steeper now as they moved up the trail, Newman first, Janet behind him. Almost at once they were out of sight of the camp, though they could smell the fire and hear the ammunition rattling off. Janet had the knife back in her scabbard. Newman had the hatchet stuck in his belt at the small of his back. He carried the carbine with both hands now, ready to fire. His hand tense on the trigger guard, listening for footsteps, fearing the sudden confrontation as the trail bent and the enemy came hurrying down toward the fire. But they met no enemy.

They stopped to rest.

"Why uphill?" Janet said.

"I figure they'd be looking for us downhill, and I didn't want to run head-on into them coming up the trail."

"Why wouldn't they be looking for us uphill?"

"Because we were downhill last they saw of us. Because like us, I bet their whole mental orientation is downhill, back toward the lake and the cottages and, you know, civilization. When we ran yesterday, which way did we go?"

"Downhill," she said.

"Right. In my mind we're on the end of a long string that stretches back to the lake but not ahead. You know?"

"Christ, you think in such elaborate pictures."

"I know. And I know you don't. I see ideas, you think them. It's one reason we argue, I guess."

"Now what?" she said.

"Now we swing around through the woods and go back down past them."

"Why didn't we do that in the first place?"

"Because we had to get away. We were in a hurry. Now we're not. Now we can sneak slowly back and cut them off below. We can't let them get out of here. They know who we are. We have to kill them all. If any one of them gets away we're as good as dead."

"I know."

"Four men," Newman said.

"I don't mind," she said.

Looking at her face in the slow-fading afternoon light, he knew she meant it. He felt the same surge of strength he'd felt before, looking at her face. The permanence of it, the hard resolve. She had an intensity of single purpose he'd never had. He could endure. But she could persist.

"You've always been tougher than me," he said.

She smiled at him. "That's because I've always had you to back me up," she said. "You never seem to understand that."

He patted her shoulder. "Well it's you and me now, babe," he said.

"We better start downhill before it gets dark," she said.

"Yeah. We don't want them ahead of us."

"What if they headed straight back for the lake as soon as they saw the fire?"

"I can't believe they would," he said as they began to work their way through the woods, swinging west of the trail and downhill. "They'd try to put out the fire. They'd try to salvage things. They'd look around for us. They'd get together and talk about what to do. It would take them a little while to realize they're stuck out here with no supplies and a full day's walk from the boats. It's almost dark. They won't want to blunder around in the dark not knowing where we are. I say they'll find someplace to hole up and take turns standing guard and wait until morning."

"I hope you're right," she said softly.

He took a small compass out of his pack. "We'll head southeast," he said, "and keep the path on our left. That way we won't get lost in the dark."

They moved as quietly as they could. It was slower going through the woods and it was dark before they were close to the campsite again. They could smell the harsh chemical smoke. He reached behind him in the darkness and took her hand. He heard human voices and they both stopped motionless. They listened. The voices went on but they were only voices. Newman couldn't hear meaning. He put his mouth against Janet's ear.

"Can you hear them?"

"Yes," she whispered, "but I can't hear what they're saying."

"Me either."

"Should we try for them now?"

"No," he whispered. "There's four of them and two of us and it's dark. We want to get them when the odds are with us. When they're in clear sight and we're not. We don't know where all of them are. It could even be a trap."

"Yes," she whispered. "You're right."

They moved along through the woods, periodically crisscrossing the trail. Every few minutes Newman stopped and checked the compass, Janet holding the flashlight with her hand over the lens and her fingers split just enough to let a small sliver of light shine on the compass. The human voices faded, and soon the chemical smell. The night sounds of the woods and the smell of the forest were all there was.

27

They were exhausted when they stopped. They had not slept since they entered the woods. They had been on their feet since sunrise, moving through thick forest. They had eaten a handful of berries. He could hear water running over rocks and remembered how thirsty he was.

"We'll stop," he said.

Janet came to a halt behind him and stood motionless, her head hanging, numb with exhaustion.

"We must be a mile or so below the camp now," Newman said. "We better sleep here or we'll fall over."

Janet stood without sound. The moon was up. It filtered, nearly full, through the trees, and Newman could see dimly around him. The trail was just to his right. Across the trail were two enormous boulders, upended, carried along and dropped there in another geologic time by the glacier. He walked closer to the boulders. Janet didn't move. Between the rocks was a space five feet wide. Newman shone his flashlight into the opening. It ran back between the two boulders for ten feet before they pressed together to form a cul-de-sac. He stepped in and straightened. The boulders were higher than his head. He could still hear the water. He stepped out from between the rocks and listened. He stepped around the rocks. There was a stream. He wondered if it were the same one. *It would have to curve back,* he thought. *But they do that, I imagine.*

He said, "Jan, you want a drink?"

She came silently over and dropped onto the ground. They lay on their stomachs and drank with cupped hands from the stream. When they finished they lay together on the ground for a moment. Then he got up and reached his hand down to her.

"Up," he said. "We'll sleep in those rocks. There's a nice place."

She lay without moving until he reached down and put his hands under her arms and pulled her up. Between the rocks pine-needles had fallen from the overhanging trees and built up a thick soft layer.

They shivered as they took off the packs.

"Getting cold," he said. They both put on the down vests and the nylon pullovers. They each ate a granola bar. She lay down and went almost at once to sleep. He felt dizzy from exhaustion, but he forced himself to stand. He went out of the refuge and with the hatchet cut several large white-pine branches from a tree behind the boulders. He took them back between the rocks and arranged them at the entrance of the refuge to shield them. Then with the carbine beside him he lay down beside her and went to sleep almost at once.

When he woke up it was raining. He looked at his watch, five thirty-six. Janet still slept motionless with her face on the pine-needles, her mouth open. The ground around him was still dry. *It must just have started,* he thought. *If we get soaked we won't get dry.* He looked out through the mouth of the refuge. Nothing moved on the trail or in the woods. Above, the sky was a uniform gray. He lay the carbine down against one of the boulders to keep the rain off it as much as possible. He unbuttoned the .32 from Janet's holster and slipped it into his pants pocket. She never stirred, her breathing steady and slow as she slept.

He took the hatchet and went out from between the rocks, moving the pine branches aside to do so. He climbed into a white spruce that towered fifty feet above the boulders. Just above the level of the boulders he began to cut branches from the tree and drop them onto the top of the rocks. He worked for nearly an hour. The hatchet was sharp and the wood was soft. He got a thick mound of spruce branches in that time. *Chris would make sure the ax was sharp,* he thought.

He slipped the hatchet back into his belt and dropped from the spruce onto the boulders. He began to lay the spruce branches in overlapping lines across the opening between the two rocks. Below him he saw Janet sit up and look up at him. It was raining harder.

He said softly, "Good morning, bright eyes."

She waved at him, sober-faced.

He laid the spruce branches across the entire opening, stopping two feet short of the point where the boulders met. The boulders were somewhat lower in front than in back, and he pointed the tips of the spruce branches in the downslant-direction.

"Is the rain still coming in?" he said to her.

"No," she said. "It's good, except at the end."

He slid off the top of the boulder and went in under his spruce-branch thatch. It was cavelike now, and darker. Janet shivered. Her teeth were chattering. Newman gave her back the .32. Thunder rolled in the distance and several seconds later lightning flashed. Newman collected dry twigs and sticks, and using a wad of toilet paper to start it he lit a fire at the narrow end of the shelter where he had not laid the roof. He bent his body over the kindling, sheltering it from the rain as he lit the paper and fed the small flame till the sticks caught. There was a slight recess at the base of the rock, and the fire was partly shielded from the rain. The smoke crawled up along the rock and slid along the face of the boulder and drifted out of the two-foot space he'd left for it. He went outside and looked. Trees masked much of the upper part of the boulders and hung over the fire hole. The smoke thinned and disappeared in the trees. It wasn't visible from the trail.

It's a risk, he thought, *but it's worth taking. We can't get soaking wet and chilled. To do this we've got to be in good shape.* He found a fallen tree and cut several lengths of firewood from it and brought it back in and put it on the fire. Reflecting off the rock the fire spread heat. Janet sat next to it hugging herself.

"Coffee would be nice," she said.

"I know it."

"Let's split a granola bar," she said.

"Okay."

"Do you think the rain will slow them up?" she said.

He chewed on his half of the bar. "I don't know. Depends whether they've found a way to get out of it,

I should think." He sat near the open end of the shelter, the carbine in his lap, looking at the trail through the screen of white-pine branches.

"Will they see the smoke?" she said.

"It gets lost in the trees," he said. "They might smell it, but they won't know where it is."

"I needed a fire," she said. "I was shaking when I woke up."

"I know. I was freezing too."

Outside the shelter the woods were silent. No bird sound. No insect sound. Nothing moved. The rain came steady and hard, dripping through the spruce branches in places. A bed of coals began to build under the fire as Newman fed it from time to time with more wood cut from the fallen tree. Nothing moved on the trail.

"What do we do," Janet said, "when we see them?"

"We shoot, or I do. You keep the pistol for back-up. It's not very accurate at any distance anyway. If we can get all four of them we're home free. If we can't we keep after them. Even if they get to the lake, remember they got no boats. It will take them a long time to walk around that lake."

She nodded. The lightning came more swiftly after the thunder now. The storm was getting closer. Newman took a book from his pack and thumbed through it. Then he stood up.

"Where're you going?" she said.

"I'm starving. I'm going to see what we can get for food."

"What's the book?"

"*A Field Guide to Survival*," Newman said. "I slipped it in the pack before we left."

"In case Chris got killed," she said.

"Yes, or separated. It's got pictures of edible plants."

"If we get out of this," she said, "you can open a Boy Scout camp."

He nodded. "Here," he said, "you take the carbine, give me the .32. I'm just going around behind the rocks."

He put the hood up on the nylon jacket, put the .32 in his pants pocket, and went out into the rain. In the stream behind the rocks were cattails. He pulled a dozen out, root and all, and brought them back into the shelter. He gave Janet back the revolver and with his jackknife cut the roots off the plants and peeled them. Then he put the twelve tubers into the ashes of the fire.

"Are they any good?" Janet said.

"Book says they are sweet and delicious," Newman said.

"I'll bet," she said.

He settled back with the carbine, watching the trail while the cattail roots roasted in the coals. Occasionally he tested them with the blade of his knife to see if they were done, and finally, when the knife slid easily in, he decided they were. He poked them out of the ashes with the knife blade and gave six to Janet. They were too hot to handle so they let them lie on a flat rock while they cooled, and Newman stared at the trail.

"You really mean that," Newman said, "about being tough because you had me to back you up?"

"Yes."

"I never fully got that sense, or the sense that you were aware of it."

"I don't know why," she said. "It seems perfectly clear."

"But you're always so manage-y. You're so . . ." He stopped and stared out at the rain-soaked trail beyond his screen of white-pine boughs, "so separate. You never seem at all dependent."

"Because I don't hold your hand or lean on your arm or run on about how much I need you?"

"Some of that wouldn't hurt," he said.

"It's not the way I am."

"Why not?"

"I suppose it has something to do with fear, fear that if I'm dependent on anything or anyone I can't control my life. It's a control issue, as they say at the consciousness groups."

"You can control me," he said.

"That scares me too. It's like the old Groucho Marx joke. I wouldn't want to depend on anyone I can control."

"Would you be more affectionate if you couldn't control me?"

"Maybe."

"But if you couldn't control me, wouldn't that scare you and make you hostile?"

"Maybe."

"Jesus Christ," he said.

"I love you, you know," she said. "I love you and I am committed to this marriage and to you. If I don't show it the way you do, that doesn't make it wrong."

"I know," he said.

"If I should love you more, maybe you should love me less. The weight of your need is heavy. The pressure of your thwarted romanticism is not pleasant, and you don't miss any chance to remind me that I'm not loving enough."

"I know."

She picked up one of the cattail roots and bit into it. He looked at her and raised his eyebrows. "Well?" he said.

"Sweet and delicious," she said. She chewed it methodically and swallowed.

He stabbed one with the blade of his jackknife and bit off half. He chewed.

"Never trust a field guide," he said and ate the other half.

"See," she said. "You don't like these damned roots and neither do I. But they're the best we've got and so we'll eat them and make the best of it."

"Half a loaf is better than none?"

She made a noncommittal gesture with her hands. "If you wish. The point is most of the time we enjoy each other very much. Be happy with that. Wanting more than you can have will spoil what you've got."

He reached out with the knife blade and stabbed another root and ate it, chewing ostensively.

"Right now," he said, "I want to kill four men."

She didn't say anything and the rain came down in sheets.

28

The rain stopped at three-twelve in the afternoon. The sun did not appear and the temperature dropped slightly. At three-fifteen he said, "They'll come now; we better be out and in a good spot."

"Why are you so sure?"

"Because they must be freezing their ass and soaking wet and hungry as hell and the first chance they get to get the hell out of the woods and get back to civilization they'll take."

"You don't think they'll be looking for us?"

"I think they'll keep an eye out, but I'll bet now they want out. They know who we are. They can get us later."

With the knife he scraped a hole in the floor of the shelter and kicked the coals of the fire into it and covered it with dirt. They slipped into the knapsacks. He looked around the small warm space once and then they left it. They went down the trail thirty yards to a place where a tree had fallen across it. They sprawled flat behind the fallen tree, to one side of the trail. Behind them the trail turned sharply east.

He took out the compass and looked at it, turning it

until he could read it. He looked southwest through the trees. Through a break in the trees he could see mountains.

"Look," he said. "See the top of that mountain? It looks like sort of a cockscomb on top?"

"It doesn't look like a cockscomb," she said.

"Well whatever it looks like to you. Study it, get it imprinted. You want to keep walking so that the mountain is about half right of you. So that you'd half-turn your head so to see it. Halfway between straight ahead and directly to your right."

"Okay."

They said nothing else but lay still watching the trail.

The wet woods dripped steadily.

Frank Marriott came first. He wore a blue plaid shirt buttoned to the neck with the collar turned up. It was wet through and his hair was plastered to his skull. In his right hand he carried a revolver with a big handle. The one he had shot Hood with. It swung at his side now, barrel pointing toward the ground. His eyes moved right and left as he came, looking in the bushes. He was walking as if his feet hurt.

Newman brought the carbine up and aimed. And waited. The blue plaid shirt seemed to enlarge as it sat on the splayed trident of the front sight. *Wait,* he thought. *Wait. If you shoot now you'll only get one. Wait until there's more than one to shoot at.* The blue shirt got bigger. *Wait, wait, wait, wait,* and his finger squeezed the trigger shut and the bullet made the material of the shirt jump as it hit Marriott in the chest. His finger squeezed again and Marriott fell backward. The gun with the big handle fell out of his hand. Behind him Richie Karl jumped for the woods to the left of the trail. Farther back the huge man and Adolph Karl stepped into the woods to the right and dropped to the ground.

Newman said, "Run," and Janet and he scrambled on the ground toward the turn in the trail. Behind them Richie Karl raised the shotgun and fired over Marriott's body in the direction the shots had come from, pumping the shotgun as fast as he could, spraying the area with an ounce and a quarter of lead shot with each pump.

As Newman and his wife reached the turn they both stood to run, and something slapped Newman in the back of the left arm. And tugged at the triceps. Then they were around the bend of the trail and running. Janet first, Newman behind her.

"Easy," he said, "watch where you're running." She slowed. "They won't come charging after us." He slowed behind her. "They don't know where we are. Don't want to turn an ankle or sprain a knee or something."

She slowed more and he slowed. They jogged for fifteen minutes, Newman listening always behind him. "Okay," he said. And they stopped.

"Did you see the others?" he said.

"Yes, they were behind. But you got the one in front."

"Bad way to do it," Newman said. "Stupid. Shouldn't have ambushed them from in front. If I'd been on the side or in an open area I could have got them all."

"You did very well," she said.

"Could have had them all. Now they'll be a lot harder."

His left arm was numb. He put his hand on it and felt the warm wet. "God," he said, "they shot me."

She looked at the back of his arm. "It's bleeding," she said. "Take off the coat and let me see."

"Not here," he said. "We got to get under cover, out of sight. Where we can watch."

"Let me tie something on it to cut down the bleeding," she said. "It won't take a minute." She took the first-aid kit from his knapsack, opened it, took out a spool of gauze bandage, and wrapped it around his arm outside the sleeve. She wrapped it as tightly as she could and then cut the bandage with her hunting knife, split the end, and tied the bandage in place.

"Okay," she said. "Let's go find a place."

"On the way up, the trail crossed a little meadow, remember? A stream ran through it and there were a lot of wild flowers and the trees were all around it. It's where the hiking sign was."

"I guess so," she said.

"Okay. We'll go there and put the meadow between us and wait for them there."

"You think they'll still come down this trail?"

"It's the only way they know. They're city, like us. They have no food. They're wet and freezing. They must be scared. They have no maps. Probably no compass. The trail's all they have. I'd stick to it."

"I hope you're right," she said.

"Even if I'm not, it's all we can do."

They walked for an hour and a half down the trail. The numbness wore out of Newman's arm. It began to throb. It was nearly dark when they reached the meadow. They crossed it and turned right along the edge of the woods and went a third of the way around the meadow and settled into a small hollow inside the cover of the woods.

Janet took the first-aid kit from her pack and placed it beside her on top of the fallen tree behind which they lay. She unwrapped the bandage on his arm, and with her knife she carefully cut the fabric on his jacket and shirt away from the wound.

"How's it look?" he said. He kept his eyes on the trail opening across the meadow.

"It's too dark to see," she said. She took the flashlight from her pack and cupping it to shield the light she looked at the wound. "It doesn't look too bad," she said. "Does it hurt?"

"Yes," he said.

"There's some like little bb's in there," she said.

"It's shot," he said. "I was hit with a shotgun."

"I think I will have to get them out," she said.

"I guess so," he said.

"Give me your jackknife," she said.

He let the carbine rest on the log as he fished his jackknife out of his right hip pocket. He handed it to her and took up the gun again.

She opened the larger blade. It had a narrow sharp point.

"Give me your lighter," she said. He handed that to her. She snapped it into flame and ran the knife blade through it. She released the lighter and slipped it into his pocket. She blew on the knife blade until it cooled. There was a smudge of black soot on it.

"What I'm going to try to do," she said, "is to pop the bb's out with the point of the knife, like you would a splinter. I'm not going to dig you."

"Okay," he said. "Go ahead."

She put the flashlight in her mouth and held it with her teeth so that the light shone on his wound and her hands were free. She carefully probed the point of the knife at the edge of a bit of shot looking black against the raw flesh. He jumped.

"Hold still," she said around the flashlight, unable to make the dental sounds.

He clamped his jaw harder and she flicked the shot out of the flesh with a quick movement of the knife blade. It didn't hurt. It was the sense of what she was doing that made him jumpy, the sense of knife blade in open wound that made the sweat begin to bead on his forehead. He was tense. He looked around at her. Saliva ran along the casing of the flashlight. Her eyebrows were down, her face taut with concentration. The light of the flashlight reflecting upward on her made her eye hollows seem deep. He noticed that she had sweat on her forehead too. He turned away and looked at the woods. She carefully and with great delicacy pried another shot fragment from the wound.

It was full dark now, the open meadow before them still gray with the memory of day, but the woods black. He jumped as she pried too deep with the knife. She murmured around the flashlight. He held still and she got another bit of lead. Across the open land an owl moved in almost soundless flight, low, looking for field mice.

She worked on his wound for twenty-five minutes. Then she put the knife down, opened a tube of antiseptic cream, smeared it on a large gauze pad, and placed the pad over the wound. She took adhesive tape from the first-aid kit and wrapped it tightly around the arm, holding the pad in place. Then she took the flashlight from her mouth.

"All there is is aspirin. Why don't you swallow a couple. Can you do it without water?"

"Yes," he said. He put the two aspirin in his mouth, tipped his head back with a sudden movement, and swallowed the aspirin.

"Here," she said, and handed him back the jack-knife. Her hands were shaking.

He put the blade into the ground to clean it and pulled it out and folded it and slipped the knife back in his hip pocket.

"Thank you," he said. His arm throbbed and he felt weak.

She shut off the flashlight and put it and the first-aid kit back in the pack.

"How do you feel?" she said.

"Not bad," he said. "It throbs, but having it band-aged right helps. Makes it feel, you know, protected."

She nodded and put her hand on the back of his neck and massaged it lightly. It was cold and getting colder. She put her hood up and tightened the drawstrings. Across the open meadow nothing moved. The owl was gone. They had become accustomed to the night sounds of the woods. It now seemed to them like quiet.

"When they get to this open place," she said, "won't they expect us to be waiting for them?"

"Yes," he said. "I would think so."

"So what will they do?"

"I wish I knew," he said. He talked without taking his eyes from the circle of wood-line. Back and forth in a slow semicircle he watched. "So far they have been stupid as hell. But they can't be that stupid. They wouldn't just walk across the open field like targets. Nobody could be that dumb."

"So what will they do?"

"Well, they don't have many choices. They have to get downhill to the lake. This trail is the only one they know. When they come to this clearing they'll have to skirt it. That means they'll be ploughing through the woods at night."

"So what will we do?"

"We'll listen," he said.

29

They lay perfectly still, shivering in the darkness, close together in the hollow just off the trail at the edge of the meadow. There was no moon and the darkness was absolute. They listened. The owl they had seen earlier still hunted and occasionally called out in his *hoo hoo hoo* sound, so like an owl was said to sound that it seemed almost contrived. They listened intensely, feeling an ache of effort along the jawline. His arm pounded steadily. There was no wind.

It was an hour before dawn. He heard a branch snap. Half hypnotized by the hours of dead-quiet concentration, he jerked as if waking up, though he had not slept. He put his hand on her arm. She patted it. She'd heard. Some twigs snapped and there was a rustling of brush. In the thick blackness it was hard to find direction. *Across the trail,* he thought. *To our right. Maybe ten, twenty yards.* He turned his body so he could point the carbine that way. There was silence. Then the sound of someone's breath, short and wheezing. A rustling movement. The wheezing breath remained constant, rasping air in and out. It was a sound of exhaustion. The twigs cracked again.

Then someone spoke, the sound shocking in the silent wilderness they'd gotten used to.

"I can't make it, Dolph," the voice said, the breath short and gasping. "I can't make it no farther."

"Shut up." It was Karl's voice. They were closer than Newman had thought. *Ten yards. Maybe less.*

"I gotta stop," the voice said. It was the one on the telephone. The huge man.

"For crissake keep your voice down," Karl said. "They might be around. They might be anywhere." Karl sounded frightened.

There was sound of movement in the brush. "Fuck'em," the huge man said. His voice shook with exhaustion. "I ain't moving."

Newman very carefully got to his feet. He stood behind the trunk of a thick oak and held the carbine chest-high, aimed at the sound of voices. He heard a scratch, smelled sulfur, and saw the flare of a match.

Karl's voice said, "Richie, are you fucking crazy . . ."

The match went out and Newman fired at the spot where it had been, the flare still an impression on his retina. He fired again, moving the barrel of the carbine an inch left. Then again, moving it two inches right. And again, two inches left. Methodically he fired in an oscillating arc centered on the place where the match had flared. He fired at waist-level. Janet crouched behind him, shielded by the tree, one hand on the inside of his right knee, the other holding her small silver revolver. He heard someone grunt. He heard Karl's voice say, "Richie?" and then, higher, "Richie?" and then gunfire returned. They were firing at the muzzle-flash of the carbine. Two slugs thumped into the tree trunk. Another splattered through the foliage to their right. He could hear Karl's voice. Cursing.

"Son of a bitch," Karl said, "son of a fucking bitch." Another bullet hit a tree somewhere behind Newman. The fifteenth shell-casing ejected from the carbine. The trigger clicked and the firing pin snapped emptily. Newman crouched behind the tree, shrugged out of the knapsack, and dug into it frantically. He found the box of shells and, fumbling in the dark, feeling the pressure of Karl's presence, he began to feed fresh ammunition into the clip. He counted, unable to see in the dark. Janet knelt with the .32 ready, looking into the dark. They were facing east and a faint tinge of gray was beginning to lessen the blackness in that direction. *Fifteen*, he said to himself, and feeling the bullets with his thumb to make sure they were in the right direction he slid the clip back up into the carbine. He tapped it home with the palm of his right hand and heard it click into place. Relief moved up along his buttocks and across his lower back. *Safety is relative*, he thought. *Now I feel safe because the gun's loaded.*

In front of them there was no noise. The absence of gunfire made the woods seem to echo with silence. The gunfire had quieted the normal forest sounds. As he got used to the silence Newman could hear two things, the sound of labored breathing and, faintly, the sound of someone running. The sky lightened a little more. Newman crouched beside Janet and put his mouth to her ear.

"We have to move," he whispered. "One of them got away and is ahead of us."

She nodded. He could now barely see her in the very early morning, but he felt her head bob, his face was so close. He started to stand. She took his arm, put her hand against his cheek, and pulled his ear to her lips.

"It's almost light," she said. "Why not wait until we can see?"

"The one that's away will get farther away," he whispered.

"You can catch him," she said. They had developed a little pattern of head-turns, so that each whispered into the other's ear.

"You think so?"

"How far can you run?" she said.

"Ten, fifteen miles."

"Can he?"

"Probably not," he said.

"Let's wait, at least until we can see."

"Okay," he said, and remained crouched beside her with the oak tree trunk shielding them. There was no more sound of feet, but they could still hear the labored breathing. It was more labored. There was a rattle to it. The sky in the east was white now. Newman could see Janet clearly beside him. There was birdsong.

"You go around that way," he whispered, and gestured to his right. "I'll come from the other side. Creep in. Be careful." He touched her hand. She smiled at him. He moved in a crouch to his left, leaving the protection of the tree, swinging around the place where the breathing came from. He held the carbine ready, his finger on the trigger, a round in the chamber. He saw the huge man first. It was he of the labored breathing. He sat with his back to a tree, a short-barreled revolver in his hand, his hands in his lap. There was blood on his throat and on the front of his shirt. His mouth was open and he seemed to be struggling to breathe. His eyes were slitted and his head would drop forward then snap back erect, like a man falling asleep at the wheel. A stubble of beard showed through the blood that had smeared up onto his chin.

Near his outstretched legs was Richie Karl. Face-down, dead. *Bullet went in the front, came out the back*, Newman thought. *Don't seem to mind*, he thought. *Doesn't seem to bother me. Get used to anything*. Beyond Richie Karl he saw Janet moving behind some sapling birch, then she stepped out from behind the saplings and stood next to the huge man.

He raised his head, jerking it up again in that peculiar motion. He squinted at her. He moved his right hand. The gun fell from it. He didn't seem to notice.

"Remember me?" she said.

He made a croaking noise.

"Remember tying me up and gagging me?" she said.

He moved his right hand again. She aimed the nickel-plated .32 revolver at his temple and pulled the trigger. A small black hole appeared in his temple and he slumped against the tree. The labored breathing stopped.

"I hope you went to hell," she said. She still held the revolver straight out ahead of her, pointed as it had been.

"Jesus," Newman said. He walked to her and pushed her arm down to her side. She didn't resist but neither was her arm limp. With one hand on each shoulder he turned her away, and then, with his arm around her waist, he moved her to the trail. Behind them the woods closed. The dead men were no more. Ahead of them the trail led gently downward. Toward the water. Out of the woods.

"One more," he said.

"Yes."

The sun appeared above the edge of the trees in the eastern sky, the top rim of it. And the woods, while shadowy, seemed pleasant and warm after the storm. They walked in silence along the trail for a quarter of a mile.

"You are going to have to run him down," she said.

"Without you?"

"You know I can't run like you can."

"You can go several miles."

"I'll have to carry your pack, unless you want to run with it on."

He shook his head. They stopped.

"If he gets away it means our death," she said. "It means our daughters' death, probably, it means the destruction of everything you've ever cherished. We've come this far. We've almost won. You'll have to do it."

His arm hurt. It had hurt all along, but in the fire fight in the darkness he'd forgotten. It throbbed and the pain ran into his shoulder and neck.

Janet said, "I can't chase him. I'm exhausted. I probably couldn't, even if I weren't." She spoke very quietly, standing right in front of him, her face close to his.

"Yes," he said. He felt heavy and slow. His legs felt weak and stiff. He was in pain. He edged the knapsack down over the wound in his arm and dropped it on the ground. He slipped off the nylon pullover and rolled it tightly and, squatting, put it into the pack. He slipped out of the down vest, rolled it tightly, and put it into the pack. Then he stripped off his shirt and stowed it.

"You've lost weight," she said.

He handed her the hatchet and she slipped it into her belt.

"You take the carbine," he said. She took it. He took from her the .32 gun and holster and strapped it to his belt, in back, near the small of his back. He was naked to the waist, shivering in the early sunlight. He had on near-white corduroy pants, and boots that laced up over the ankle. They were expensive and weighed very little. He put two granola bars in his pants pocket.

"What if he's waiting ahead, like we did?" she said.

He shrugged. "If he is, he is. You're right. I got no choice."

"Maybe he won't be."

"Maybe. He doesn't know how many of us there are. His whole party's been shot. He's alone in the woods. He must be scared. I hope he'll just run."

"I'm glad we destroyed the boats," she said.

"I wish we'd destroyed the canoe. If he finds it we've lost."

"He won't," she said.

He looked again at her. She still had the green nylon pullover on, the hood over her head, the drawstring tight. It framed her face like a nun's habit. There was no makeup left, and her face was gray with fatigue. But there was no uncertainty in the face. He'd looked at the same face with the strong planes and the wide mouth for almost as long as he could remember. Without makeup a few freckles showed against her pale skin. There were deep parenthetical lines around her mouth. Deeper than he remembered. He was enough taller than she was so that she tilted her head slightly to look at him.

"You can do this," she said. "He won't find the canoe. You will catch him."

There were tiny lines at the corners of her eyes, a tiny red mark under her right eye. He could see the pores in her skin.

"You can," she said.

He nodded. "Here I go," he said. And turned and began to jog down the trail away from her, toward the lake.

30

He jogged slowly. He wasn't used to running in boots and they felt heavy on his feet. But he remembered running in boots in the Army. *I'll get used to it.* He watched the trail ahead of him: it was narrow and it turned frequently. There were fallen branches occasionally, and tree roots that reared here and there above ground, and rocks, some as big as softballs. What seemed easy to walk on became dangerous to run on. He knew that. The years of jogging had left him so sensitive to footing that he could feel the difference between running on sidewalk and running in the street. *Street's better. More give. Smooth. Shows what we care about in our culture.* He took short steps. Running, even running slowly, increased his sense of the trail's downward pitch. He felt clumsy and stiff, the joints awkward-feeling, and slow. His breathing was ragged. *I'll never make a mile,* he thought, and thought how often he'd said that. He always felt this way when he started. As if today he couldn't do it. But he pressed on and always he loosened up and the breath came easy and he found he could make it. *It'll happen this time too,* he thought.

The sun rose higher. In places among the trees a thin fog steamed up from the wet leaves. The pitch of the trail flattened slightly. As he ran, his eyes moved steadily back and forth across the trail into the woods on either side. He could almost feel the threat of gunfire, the bullet hitting him in the chest, a massive thump. A green garter snake with black stripes glided across the path in front of him, moving as if without volition. He began to feel warmer. He stayed on the pace, slow, easy, his arms held slightly above his waist moving in rhythm with his steps. When he'd first begun to run regularly, he remembered, he'd worked on the rhythm, getting the feet to move steadily, and the arms. When he'd been teaching his daughters he used to emphasize it: "Get the rhythm down," he'd told them. "Later it will be much easier to run if you run in an organized way. If you look good or at least better." They hadn't stuck with the running, though, and had never got beyond the stage where their arms and legs moved in ragged asymmetry. Above him two sparrows chased a crow, darting about it in flight, looking ludicrously small next to the great black scavenger. But the crow fled, and the sparrows pursued. *Watch the path* he said to himself. *Twist your ankle and you might as well be dead. Never mind the fucking birds.* He was conscious as he jogged of the weight of the revolver banging against his coccyx. It was the best place for it. It would be more bothersome anywhere else. He began to loosen. His legs felt freer, stretched out more. His arms moved easier, he felt sweat begin to form on his bare back. He felt lighter. *I probably have lost weight. I ought to. Haven't eaten anything to speak of in . . .* He couldn't remember how long they'd been in the woods. A ground squirrel crossed his path, its tail out straight behind it, its feet moving very rapidly. He remembered how he used to try to keep his cat from killing chipmunks as a boy and how determined the cat was, dodging his broom, circling back to torment and toy with the half-crippled chipmunk, too quick for him to grab, until his father had told him not to interfere, that even if he saved the chipmunk its spine was probably broken and it would die a lingering death anyway. At night the cat slept on his bed. The fall of his feet sounded in his listening mind like the beat behind music. It always did, and songs moved aimlessly through his head, *do wah, let's take the A-train, the fastest the quickest way to get to Harlem.* Windshield wipers did that too, always sounded like the Garryowen, he thought. He was now sweating evenly, his face and chest wet, a trickle collecting in the gully between his pectoral muscles. The sound of the air moving past his ears was pleasant. The sun was bright now, and warm. His breathing was steady, his heart pumped easily. His arms swung free, *like some of those ads in* Runner's World, he thought, seeing himself from a remote vantage, small, shirtless, running through the enormous forest toward a distant lake. *Could do an article on the training effect of homicidal necessity.* *"How my Nikes helped me run a man down and kill him," by Aaron Newman. "We think you'll find it a fascinating new look at cross-country running."* A branch leaned across the trail and he ducked under it, pushing it aside with his forearm. Through the trees ahead he caught a sudden shine. The lake. It was almost as if he'd come upon a scene from his childhood. He felt a little hollow seeing the gleam of the lake through the fringe of coloring leaves. Then the trail turned and he didn't see it, and the trail turned again and he did, the sun dancing off it in odd and random splatters of light as the water moved. Then he was at the lake, his breath coming in large, clear drafts, still breathing through his nose. He stopped.

Along the lake the snowmelt rise in spring and the summer parch of August had left a belt of rough and sandless beach ten feet wide where there were no trees and no topsoil. The belt circled the lake. A mile away from Newman, Adolph Karl walked and occasionally ran along this belt, looking back regularly over his shoulder. He couldn't see Newman yet, standing in the shadow of the trees. Newman took one of the granola bars from his pocket and unwrapped it and threw the wrapper on the ground. *In an emergency,* he thought, *litter.* The granola bar seemed to absorb into his body tissue. Still chewing on the bar, he began to run after Karl.

It was harder running here. No longer downhill, and very uneven underfoot. There were fallen trees to get over or around, rocks, brush, areas of soft mud. *Don't have to move fast, just faster than him.* Karl looked back and saw Newman. Karl reached into the pocket of his red plaid coat and brought out a .45 automatic. Newman saw him stop, turn, raise the gun, and fire. The bullet whanged off a rock far in front of Newman. Newman kept running, varying his gait and direction, running in a weaving path to make him a harder target. He tried to crouch, but it was hard to keep pace crouching. He took out his own small revolver. But didn't shoot. Karl after one shot turned and began to run. He ran badly. *No rhythm,* Newman thought. *Too fast. He can't keep it up.* Karl's arms moved awkwardly and without synchronization. He slipped and fell once. He got up looking back over his shoulder and ran again. His feet pointed out to the side. He seemed to Newman to limp on his right foot. Newman kept his pace. Ahead of him, now slightly more than half a mile, Karl pushed harder, running full tilt across the cluttered and difficult rim of the lake. He fell, sprawling full-length. The .45 sprawled ahead of him. He scrambled after it on hands and knees, retrieved the gun and, still on his knees, turned, aimed the .45 with both hands, and squeezed off a shot. It was still too far. Newman didn't hear the bullet. He kept his pace. Free of the trees the early fall sun beat down strong and solid against his chest and face. He squinted. The smell of the lake mixed with the smell of its margin. Karl was on his feet, limping more clearly, hobbling as he ran, looking back more often, and still Newman came, the footfalls steady, rhythmical, ". . . *the A-train, do wah, you'll get where you're going in a hurry,*" his eyes on the ground and then on Karl, alternating the ground and Karl as he watched where he ran and watched what he ran for. It was almost hypnotic, in the sun and the quiet, by the edge of the lake in the early autumn. *A man alone running after quarry,* he thought. *Opus one, it's not for Sammy Kaye, hey, hey, hey.* A new rhythm fitted into the steady thump of his feet. As he ran, each foot hit the ground just before the arch, on the back of the ball, and almost at once thereafter the heel touched. He had closed the gap. He was a quarter of a mile from Karl now. Karl ran in spurts, hard briefly and then slower and then, looking back and seeing Newman closing, he'd run hard and the distance between them would increase, but he couldn't sustain and then he'd falter and the gap closed more than before. Newman felt stronger, as if he could run on at this pace until he grew old and died. Even with the bad footing he felt irresistible, "*with the ruthless and irresistible deliberation of a locomotive,*" he thought. He smiled. *Always the literati,* he thought, "*not even a mortal beast but an anachronism indomitable and invincible out of an old dead time, a phantom, epitome and apotheosis of the old wild life.*" He laughed, a short "Hah!" and began to jog faster, like a train, its momentum picking up. Karl scrambled across the broken trunk of a dead tree whose upper branches trailed in the lake. *I'm coming, Karl,* he said silently. *I'm coming, you son of a bitch.* Karl fell again as he climbed down on the other side of the fallen tree, and stayed down for a moment this time. Newman was two hundred yards away. Karl staggered as he got to his feet, nearly fell, and turned to look back at Newman. He started; Newman was much closer. Karl steadied himself and aimed the .45 with both hands, his elbows resting on the trunk of the fallen tree. Newman ran a sinuous course as he came. Karl aimed. Newman saw the gun, saw Karl steady it on the log. "Fuck you," he said aloud, though Karl couldn't hear him. He straightened as he ran, and stopped swerving. He ran straight at Karl, moving faster, arms pumping, the big quadriceps muscles in his thighs tightening and softening under the tight stretch of the corduroy, the sweat glistening on his upper body making the muscle definition more apparent as he ran. "Shoot me if you can, you son of a bitch," he said. Again Karl didn't hear. He sighted over the short front sight of the .45 at Newman's bounding glistening chest. Karl's hands shook. Newman was coming on, coming on, too close, he kept going off and on the sight, the gun wavered, centered, Karl pulled the trigger, and the shot went five feet to the right of Newman and two feet above his head. Newman came on now, pounding, arms pistoning, legs driving, the muscles in his neck definite and taut, the small nickel-plated five-shot Smith & Wesson revolver in his right hand glinting occasionally in the sun. He jumped over a low rock and landed without breaking stride. Karl aimed, panic flooded through him as he squeezed the trigger again, the sight square on Newman's looming chest. The hammer clicked on empty. The clip was spent. He'd never reloaded. After the fire fight in the woods, he'd simply run. Newman heard the click as he pounded on, less than a hundred yards now. He heard another click as Karl squeezed the trigger again in a kind of blind panic, and Newman laughed, loudly, and Karl heard him; it was an explosion of mirthless and savage sound. One laugh. "It's empty, you son of a bitch," Newman said, and Karl could hear him. "It's empty, you motherfucker, and I'm coming."

Karl turned and ran. It was no more than a walk. Newman was fifty yards from him. He turned toward the trees, but the banks here had eroded away and formed a flat dirt face eight feet high, laced with the exposed roots of the trees that perhaps next year would topple into the lake. Newman was closer. Karl turned and ran toward the lake. He splashed into it thigh-deep, heading straight out toward the center. Newman came in behind him in a thundering cascade of spray and footfall, driving through the water. He was five yards away. Karl stumbled forward in the water and went under. He came up gasping and Newman was beside him. As Karl's head broke water,

Newman shoved the small nickel-plated gun into Karl's face and held it. Karl could see his face with the eyes widened as far as they would and the mouth open and the nostrils flared. Newman's chest heaved steadily as he drew in air. There were welts across his face and chest where branches had slapped him and brambles had torn. He was, aside from the movement of his chest, absolutely still with the gun barrel pressed into the bridge of Karl's nose. Karl, half out of the water, sank back and sat on the bottom. The water came to his chest. He stared up at Newman as if he were in a stupor. He gasped for breath, short gasps, one after another. His face was scratched and bruised and stung. There was blood and sweat and dirt on it that the plunge into the lake had not washed away. The wet hair was thin. A lot of scalp showed through. Dimly through the rust-colored lake water the faint glint of the useless .45 showed, still clutched in Karl's right hand, resting against the bottom of the lake. High above them a fish hawk circled in the sky, slowly, in narrowing circles, without haste, as if time were of no consequence and the present would last forever.

31

Neither of them spoke. Karl stared up at Newman from his sunken eyes without expression. He was shivering. Newman felt the steady thump of his own heart and the sense of blood moving swiftly through his body. Karl made no move to avoid the pressure of the gun barrel. He made no move at all. Neither did Newman. The fish hawk widened out his circle again above them, searching, drifting on his angular six-foot wingspan. Somewhere in the ringing silence a fish broke water and the hawk swerved and dropped. Karl leaned slightly backward in the water and very slowly got his feet beneath him and inched up out of the water until he was standing. Newman's gun had followed him as he rose, the barrel still pointed at the space between Karl's eyebrows. Karl backed away a step. Newman didn't move. The blankness began to ebb from Karl's face. He was still shivering. He still held the empty .45 in his right hand. Water dripped from it as he stood. Karl's breath was less frantic. His eyes were bloodshot and watery. He took a step to his right, Newman moved the gun, keeping it on Karl's face. Karl took another step. Newman moved the gun.

Karl leaned forward. Newman bent his elbow and brought the gun back toward him slightly. Halfway across the lake behind them the fish hawk rose with a smallmouth bass in his talons, banked toward the west, and flew down the lake and disappeared into the trees.

Karl swung his empty .45 at Newman's gun hand and hit it, and both weapons, one still loaded, skittered across the lake top and sank. Newman's right hand hurt. It was a numb pain. Karl lurched forward through the water and tried to knee Newman in the groin. Newman turned in time and took the knee against his thigh. Karl clawed at Newman's face with his left hand. With his right he hit Newman in the throat. Newman made a choking noise and staggered away from him. Karl punched him again and Newman half-turned and staggered away another step. Karl jumped at him and landed on his back and wrapped his arm around Newman's neck. The impact made Newman drop to his knees. Newman tucked his chin in and Karl couldn't get his arm under Newman's jaw and against his throat. With both arms Karl squeezed.

Newman felt the pressure build in his head. His sight glazed red. He heaved himself upright, Karl still hanging on. With his feet spread, knee-deep in water, Newman reached up and pried one of Karl's fingers free and bent it backward until Karl let go of his neck. He made a massive shrugging motion with his shoulders and back and dumped Karl into the water. His heart was pounding and the blood thumped in his head. Karl stood up. Newman got hold of his neck with one hand and his shirt front with the other and began to bend him backward, pulling on the shirt front, pushing on the neck. Karl was a big-boned, angular man. But he was exhausted and he was out of shape. Newman bent him backward slowly. Karl tried for Newman's groin again but was off-balance and struggling and there was no force to the knee. Again Newman took it on his thigh. His right hand squeezed into Karl's neck. He could feel the cartilage and tissue move under his fingers. He dug in. The bench presses were paying off. The years of repetitions with two-hundred-pound barbells—ten reps, wait, ten more reps, wait, ten more reps—had left him with strength that Karl couldn't match, and here, desperate and frightened and bursting with anger, the strength finally mattered. His pectoral muscles bulged, the triceps indented at the top of his arms. The muscles of his forearms were rigid against his skin, his neck was thick with effort. The trapezius muscles swelled his shoulders.

Karl was choking. He made slight cawing sounds as Newman bent him back. The bandage on Newman's left arm was undone and flapping. The wound had begun to seep blood and it trickled down his arm. Karl scratched and clawed at Newman's face, trying to gouge his eyes. Newman increased his pressure. He grunted and then exhaled explosively, the way he did when he lifted weights. Karl gave way. He went backward into the water and Newman came down on top of him, his hands still locked on the throat and shirt front. He pressed Karl back against the bottom of the lake. The bleeding wound in his arm made the water near him slightly pink. Karl's legs thrashed and his hands stopped digging at Newman's face and went to Newman's hands. Under the water he tried to pry Newman's grip from his neck. He dug at Newman's fingers, but Newman increased the pressure. Pressing down more. He could feel the swell of strength in his back and shoulders, feel the force in his arms. There was triumph in the feeling, as his muscles swelled and held. Beneath the water Karl made no sound. He arched his body, thrashed his legs, dug with his fingers at Newman's grip. Newman remained as rigid as a boulder. Sweat stood on his forehead. He bit his lower lip with effort and it drew blood and that dripped down his chin and added its pink tinge to the water already touched with the blood from his wounded arm. His eyes were closed. In that position they held. Karl's struggles slowed. They stopped. He was still on the bottom. Newman still held him against the pebbled bottom while his arms no longer clawed but hung limp and moved slightly in the eddying water, held him several minutes after it was necessary, held him after he had died, held him as if he were unable to let go and would hold him until the lake rose in spring and covered them both. Then slowly his body began to unclench. He relaxed his hands, though he still bent forward pressing lightly against Karl's chest. The trapezius muscles eased, the cords in his forearms smoothed. He rocked back, away from Karl's body, and sat on his haunches, still astride him. He took in air in a long shuddering breath and let it out through closely pursed lips in a slow hiss.

It was fifteen minutes before Newman could stand. His body shook. He staggered as he turned toward shore and began to wade. The blood trickled down his left arm and his chin. There were more scratches and gouges on his face. And five parallel red scratches on his chest where Karl had dragged desperate fingernails just before he died.

He got to shore and found a rock near the bank and trembling sat down on the rock with his back to the bank. His wet, half-naked body was cold. There was a small breeze. It was September. He shivered. He clasped his arms around himself and sat, trembling with exhaustion, shaking with emotion, shivering with cold. He sat that way for an hour, until Janet came out of the woods and found him.

32

Bundled in his down vest and nylon parka, but still shivering, Newman waited in silence while Janet found the canoe. He was almost entirely inside himself as they paddled it out onto the still surface of the lake and headed straight across toward the cabin. His arm hurt as he paddled but he showed no sign of it, and the pain barely registered. Halfway across they let the canoe drift and dropped everything but the first-aid kit and the clothes they wore overboard. The carbine was the last thing. He didn't like to drop it. It was compact and shapely. It felt good in his hand. He held it barrel-down for a moment at arm's-length and then let it go. It slid smoothly into the water and sank.

"It's funny," he said.

"What is?"

"To be without a gun. I don't feel right."

She smiled. "You didn't need a gun at the end."

"I couldn't shoot," he said. "I wanted to. I knew I had to, but I couldn't, not up close, with him looking at me."

"You did what you had to," she said.

He shifted the paddle as the canoe began to veer

off course. Even with the wounded arm he was so much stronger than she was that the canoe wouldn't hold straight if he didn't compensate.

"And you did it alone," she said.

The sun was directly overhead, and there was no wind. The lake was slick and the canoe moved over it as if without friction.

"Without me," she said.

He could see the float in front of the cabin now, and the small wharf that slanted up from it. The foliage had begun to change and there were scatters of gold and red in the shoreline forest.

"When we came back from Korea," he said, "we came into San Francisco Bay under the Golden Gate Bridge and they tied in the ship's speaker-system to a disc jockey in San Francisco, so that before we even saw land we heard American radio, and commercials, and when we went up the bay we could look up the hilly streets into San Francisco and see American buildings and people and cars." His voice was as flat and still as the surface of the lake. She looked back at him over her shoulder. He wasn't looking at her. He was looking past her at the dock. She turned back and dug in her paddle.

They left the paddles in the bottom of the canoe when they docked. His arm hurt when he had to put weight on it to climb from the skittish canoe. On the dock they stood together. He looked back across the lake. On the far side the woods were unbroken and uniform, patches of color blotching the green. The lake remained smooth and calm. It had healed over the wake of the canoe as it had closed over the carbine, as it had closed over Adolph Karl.

"It's pretty," he said.

"Yes."

"From a distance," he said.

"Looking back," she said.

They turned toward the cabin. He swayed slightly. She put her hand on his shoulder. "Are you all right?" she said.

"Yeah. It's just that I'm tired. Fighting makes you tired. And I haven't eaten. And I suppose I've lost some blood, and I feel a little dizzy."

"Come on," she said. "We'll go to the cabin and you can lie down."

He was very slow as they walked up the path. She walked close beside him although she didn't touch him. The side door was unlocked. They went in. It was empty and still and strange. He stood swaying in the center of the room, his teeth chattering.

"Get out of the wet clothes," she said. "And lie down. I'll put a sleeping bag over you. And I'll make a fire."

He nodded. She went to the bedroom for a sleeping bag. Only the three bags and the full refrigerator gave sign that they'd ever been there. *Chris was careful*, she thought.

Newman with his head down, still fully dressed, stepped uncertainly toward the couch. When his shins hit the edge of it he swayed forward and fell face-down on the couch. He didn't move. When Janet came back with the sleeping bag he was asleep with his mouth open, breathing evenly. A fire was laid in the fireplace. She put down the sleeping bag and lit the fire. Then she went to the couch. She took off his boots and socks. There were large holes in both socks at the big toe and on the balls of both feet. She threw the socks into the fireplace. She worked her hands in

under his stomach and got his belt unbuckled and his
fly unzipped. Then she inched the wet pants down
over his thighs and finally worked them off. She did
the same with his underwear. She unzippered the
sleeping bag, spread it over Newman's half-dressed
and motionless body, picked up his pants and underwear, and went to the bathroom.

In an alcove off the bathroom was a washer and
dryer. She let the water run into it. When it was full
she added soap and dropped his pants and underwear
into it. Then she stripped off her own clothes and put
them in. She shut the top of the washer and walked
naked to the shower. With the water as hot as she
could take it she stood under the shower. She shampooed her hair twice. She lathered her whole body
with soap and rinsed and did it again. There was still
grime around her ankles and she squatted in the
shower with the hot water cascading over her to
lather and massage them a third time. When she was
through the water rinsed them clean. She stepped
from the shower into the cold bathroom, shivering.
She had no other clothes and she wrapped the one
towel around her as best she could and walked to the
living room. The fire was dancing now and the living
room was warm and rich with the smell of hardwood
burning. Her husband had not moved.

She stood close to the fire naked and rubbed herself dry. She didn't like being naked. It made her afraid.
Whenever she was naked she felt people were staring at her. She looked down at her naked body. The
scratches on her belly had faded. She couldn't see
them anymore. Her hair, still wet despite toweling,
was in tight ringlets. When it dried it would soften.
She heard the washer thump to the end of its cycle.

She walked, still clutching the towel to cover her front, to the washer and transferred the wet clothes to the dryer. It was awkward to do holding the towel with one hand. But she managed. Still holding the towel she went to the kitchen. In the refrigerator there were beer and wine, in the freezer there was steak. In the cabinet there were canned baked beans and a bottle of bourbon and a loaf of rye bread, unsliced, in a cellophane sack, tied with a small green wire twist. She took the steak from the freezer. She took the bourbon down from the cabinet, got a glass, put two ice cubes in it, and filled it with bourbon. She drank half of the bourbon, shuddered, and put the glass on the counter. In a cabinet under the sink she found a casserole and got it out. She took down two large cans of baked beans with pork. There was a hand can-opener in the drawer. She got it out and tried to open the beans and hold the towel. She couldn't.

"Shit," she said. She let the towel drop and opened the beans. Standing at the counter, she ate half of them cold, with a piece of bread. She put the rest in the casserole in the gas oven on warm. She left the steak thawing on the counter and took the bourbon bottle and the glass. She looked at the towel on the floor, but her hands were full, so she walked naked into the living room and sat naked in an armchair close to the fire and began to sip the bourbon. The heat of it moved through her and the heat of the fire thickened around her.

The fire hissed softly. At one end of the nearest logs, moisture bubbled out and dropped to the coals and turned into steam and disappeared. The lower logs began to sag, reddening into coals. She got up and put two more logs on the fire. She walked over to look down at her husband. He was as she had left him. Motionless except for the slow, easy rise and fall of his upper body as he breathed. Saliva had trickled from his open mouth, and there was a small wet circle on the sofa pillow. She still had the glass in her hand, almost empty now. She made a small gesture with it and raised it slightly toward him. "Not bad," she said out loud. He didn't move and she drank the rest of her drink. There was a small ice cube left in the bottom of the glass. She tipped it into her mouth and sucked on it, moving it from one cheek to the other as she stood watching him sleep. Then she went back to the kitchen, got more ice, went to the living room, poured more bourbon, and sat naked by the fire looking at the coals and sipping the bourbon.

33

When Newman woke up he could smell food. He felt the sudden tingle of saliva in his mouth at the thought of it. The room was warm and half lit with the moving gleam of the fire. He sat up. His right thigh hurt where Karl had kneed him, trying for the groin. His neck was sore. His forearms and the high muscles behind his shoulders were sore. He swung his feet to the floor.

Across the room by the fire, in a chair, he saw Janet. She wore no clothes. She sipped very small sips from a large glass full of ice and bourbon. She held the glass with both hands and didn't sip often. She looked at him as he sat up.

He said, "Hello."

She said, "Hello."

He said, "You don't seem to be wearing any clothes."

She said, "I washed our stuff and took a shower. There was nothing to put on."

He said, "I smell food."

She said, "I put some beans in the oven, and there's steak."

"Haven't you eaten?"

"I had some beans. I waited to eat the steak with you."

He still sat on the couch, looking at her. "You don't usually sit around with your clothes off," he said.

"There's beer in the refrigerator," she said. "You want any?"

He said, "Yes."

She said, "I'll get it for you, but take a shower first. You smell like a porcupine."

"How the hell do you know what a porcupine smells like?"

She giggled. "It smells just like you," she said. "That's how I know."

"For crissake," he said, "you're half zonked." There was pleasure in his voice.

"Go take your shower, porcupine breath," she said. "You're sitting around bare-ass and half zonked."

"There's a towel on the kitchen floor," she said and took another tiny sip of bourbon.

The soap stung the scratches on his face, but he washed his face carefully anyway, rubbing the lather into the scratches to get them clean. The wounded arm stung but he washed that too, tightening against the pain. He washed and rinsed and lathered and rinsed again and shampooed his hair twice. There was no toothbrush but he rubbed his teeth with salt on the ball of his forefinger and rinsed his mouth in the shower's stream, gargling and spitting. When he got out of the shower and toweled off he looked at himself in the mirror. He was much slimmer. The roll of fat around his middle was gone. His stomach lay flat between his hip bones. *Great diet,* he thought. *A few days in the wilderness and all baby fat is gone.*

He hung the towel on the back of the bathroom door and walked to the living room. She handed him a beer. He popped open the can and drank a sip. It was cold and it felt clean as it coursed through him. He hadn't had a drink for days. Janet got the first-aid kit and rebandaged his arm. Then she sat back in her chair with the big lowball glass held in both hands, clinking the ice and looking into the fire. It was night. The fire was the only light in the room. She sipped the bourbon. He drank from his can of beer. A spark popped from the fire out onto the hearth, and sputtered and faded out.

She looked up at him across the rim of the glass. He sipped the rest of the beer and put the can on the mantel. She put the half-drunk glass of bourbon on the floor and stood up. They both stood still five feet apart. She swayed very slightly.

"I don't want you to think this means more than it does," she said. She took two steps toward him and put her arms around his neck and raised her face to his. Her mouth was slightly open. Her lips were wet from bourbon and ice and it made them shiny. He put his arms around her waist, his hands one on top of the other in the small of her back.

"This doesn't mean that I'm going to be different," she said. Her speech slurred very slightly. He pressed her against him and put his head down and kissed her open mouth. Under his lips it opened wider. Her body arched back, her arms tightened around his neck. He put his tongue into her mouth. She touched the tip of it with hers and opened her mouth wider. Her body loosened and relaxed, she went limp against his arms, pulling him toward the floor with her weight. Her arms fell away and she seemed boneless. He raised his head slightly to look at her. She lay back against his arms, limp, her mouth open, her eyes half closed. Her breathing was short and shallow. She ran the tip of her tongue along the inner edge of her lower lip. Carefully he eased her to the floor. She was without volition. When she was on the floor she let her legs fall open, her hands nearly by her sides, looking up at him still with half-closed eyes. Her breath was even shorter and there was a faint sound to it, a murmur. He rested on his right elbow beside her, lying on his side, close to her. She turned her head toward him but made no other movement. He kissed her again. Her mouth was loose. He put his left hand against her cheek and moved it down along her neck to her breast. He moved his hand on her breast. He rubbed the nipple softly with the ball of his forefinger. The murmur in her breath became a soft groan. She shifted slightly and closed her eyes entirely, her hands still lying motionless beside her, palms up, fingers slightly curled. He put his mouth to her breast. She tipped her head back slightly and put her right hand up and rested it gently on the back of his head. She groaned softly. He moved his left hand down her body across her stomach. She arched her pelvis up at him and pushed his head more firmly against her breast. He slipped his right hand beneath her shoulders and moved his left hand between her thighs. She groaned more loudly. She moved her legs farther apart. Both her arms were around him now, and they remained in that balance between tension and lassitude as the glow from the fire softened their movements and warmed them. In a while she shifted and helped him as he slid between her legs. She said, "Yes," once and raised her head and shoulders slightly to kiss him as their bodies moved in intuitive union.

When it was over and they were spent she looked up at him in the rose-tinged semidarkness and said, "I love you very much."

"I love you," he said. There were tears on his face. Then he put his face down beside hers and they lay still on the floor in front of the fire with their arms around each other, still pressed together. A log shifted as the center burned through and the two halves slowly settled toward the center.

"Don't expect too much next time," she said. Her eyes were closed and she lay with her head resting on his right arm.

"I'll take what I can get," he said. His voice was hoarse.

She opened her eyes and looked at him without moving her head. Then she said, "The floor is quite hard."

"True."

"Let's get up and eat."

"Okay," he said. "Let's get dressed before we eat, though. I'm freezing my ass off."

The clothes were still warm from the dryer when they put them on. His shirt had gone overboard with the knapsack. He wore the vest over his bare upper body. She sipped her bourbon while she set the table in front of the fire. He forked the half-thawed steak onto the swing-out grill in the fireplace. It began to sizzle almost at once as the flame touched it. The coals were thick on the firebed now, and the fireplace was very hot. She brought him another can of beer.

He drank from it. She put the casserole of beans on a hot pad on the table. They were bubbling softly. She put out the rye bread, some ketchup, some pickles, two dinner plates, knives and forks. He turned the steak on the grill, feeling the heat blistering his hand as he did. She finished setting the table and sat in one of the chairs and sipped her bourbon. The steak sizzled for three more minutes on the grill and then he put it on a plate and brought it to the table. He cut it in two pieces with his pocket knife, gave one half to her, and put the other half on his own plate. Then he sat down and they ate.

They ate in silence. The food occupied them completely. And as they ate it they thought of when they had eaten a granola bar for dinner.

"It's lovely to eat," she said.

He put some ketchup on his beans. "Yes," he said. "One of the great meals."

They finished eating and wiped the plate clean with the last of the bread. He went to the kitchen and brought out coffee in thick china mugs with pictures of vegetables on them.

"What do we do now?" Janet said.

Newman sipped the coffee. "We drive Chris's car home, time it to arrive at night, put it in his garage in the dark, go home to our house, and take up our lives again. There's nothing to connect us. The rent's paid in advance on this place. When the week's up, we're gone. The owner will think nothing of it. Before we leave tomorrow I'll wipe the place for fingerprints."

"Everywhere? That's a big order." She sipped at her coffee, holding the mug at chin level and breathing in the steam.

"No, just refrigerator, chrome sink-handles, bathroom and toilet handles, that stuff. They can't pick anything up off fabric and floors and stuff."

"How do you know about fingerprints?"

"It stands to reason," he said. "It's got to be something smooth that the oils of the fingertips will leave a trace on, right?"

She shook her head. "I have no idea about fingerprints," she said. "I'll have to trust you. How's the arm? It looked clean when I bandaged it."

"Seems pretty good. I looked at it in the shower. I don't see any infection. It's not swollen or very red. We'll keep an eye on it. If it gets worse I'll go to some suburban hospital emergency room and give a phony name. Happens all the time."

"And how in hell do you know that?"

"I asked Teddy Schroeder. He interned in the emergency room at United Hospital. I was doing a book where the question came up. He says that's no sweat. They report it to the police but it's routine, and they don't ask for ID or anything."

She smiled. "You do know things. The shelter in the woods. I know you've never built a shelter before."

"Yeah, but I've carpentered. I have built a lot of things. There's logic to things. You build one thing you learn the logic of building. How else would you make a shelter there?"

"I don't know. But it worked. You made it work."

"Thank you," he said.

"How do you feel?" she said.

"Physically? Or emotionally?"

"Both," she said. "You've had to do an awful thing and it was terrible and frightening and you did all of it. How does it make you feel?"

He drank some of his coffee. "Strong," he said.

"Strong and close-knit, and not very much thinking. You know. I don't want to think very much. I want to work on intuition and feeling and eat what tastes good and drink what's cold and do a lot of screwing and sleeping and wearing clean clothes."

They were quiet, drinking coffee, looking at the fire.

"I couldn't have gone into the woods without you," he said. "And I could never have gotten out."

"We went together," she said. "And came out the same way."

"More together," he said. "Much more together."

"Don't do that," she said. "Don't start expecting too much."

He smiled at her, the smile widening across his face as if it would distort. Even in the dimness of the firelight his eyes gleamed.

"I don't expect anything," he said. "I take what comes. And we make do."

Epilogue

It was two weeks before Thanksgiving and the wound in Newman's arm was only a smooth red scar when Vincent and Croft came to call. They came in a dark blue Chevrolet with a whip antenna but no other markings and parked under Newman's ancient maple tree in the early evening.

Croft rang the bell and Newman answered. His face was blank when he saw the two policemen, and he said, "What can I do for you gentlemen?"

Croft said, "We'd like to come in and talk for a few minutes."

Vincent said, "We're not here to arrest you."

Newman said, "That's good. Come in. We're having dinner. Would you be willing to sit and have a drink or something with us while we finish?"

Vincent said, "Sure."

Janet Newman, still dressed from work in a black pantsuit with vest, and black boots with high spike heels, was eating linguine with clam sauce at the kitchen table across from Newman's now empty place. There was a bottle of Graves and two glasses. Janet sipped some wine, put the glass down, and smiled at them.

"This is my wife, Janet," Newman said. "These are state policemen. Corporal Croft and Lieutenant Vincent."

Janet smiled more brightly and said, "How do you do. Can we get you some wine or coffee? Piece of pie? Have you eaten?"

"We've eaten," Vincent said, "thank you. I'd be happy to have a drink though. Bobby?"

Croft said, "Yeah, me too. I'll take a beer if you've got one."

"Scotch," Vincent said. "Neat. No ice, nothing."

Newman got them each a drink. Croft declined a glass. They sat at the kitchen table.

"Remember Adolph Karl?" Croft said.

"The guy I identified and changed my mind?" Newman said.

"The very one," Croft said. Vincent sipped his Scotch carefully and tipped his head back slightly to savor it as he swallowed. "Good Scotch," he said.

"He's dead," Croft said. "Somebody apparently drowned him in a lake in Maine."

Newman ate some pasta and drank half a glass of wine.

"I assume you're not very unhappy," Newman said. "As I recall, you didn't think well of him."

"He was a scum bag," Croft said. "Excuse me, ma'am."

"I hear worse from him every day," Janet said. She smiled at Croft.

"Thing is, somebody seems to have wiped out practically his whole social circle, up there in Maine. A ranger in the National Forest up there found them scattered all around. His two sons, his bodyguard, and one of his associates, all gunned down here and there."

Newman nodded. He ate some salad.

"Nobody's hysterical with grief," Croft said. He drank from the beer can. "They were all maggots and whoever burned them did the world a favor. Interesting thing was, another guy got killed up there, guy named Hood. Chris Hood. Know him?"

"Of course. He lives right back of us."

"Yeah," Croft said. "That sort of got our attention."

"Meaning?"

"Meaning the coincidence. Here you think Karl did a murder and then you think he didn't, then a guy who lives right next to you gets killed in the same woods with Karl." Croft drank more beer. He put the can down and belched softly. " 'Scuse me," he said.

Vincent took another small sip of Scotch.

Newman had finished eating. He sipped his wine.

Janet Newman was still eating. She speared a mushroom slice from her salad bowl and put it in her mouth.

Vincent said to Newman, "You've lost some weight haven't you?"

"Yes, about twenty pounds."

"Look good," Vincent said.

"That's terrible about Chris," Janet said. "We were quite good friends."

"But you haven't seen him in the last month or so, have you," Croft said.

"No," Janet said. "I assumed he'd gone hunting. He does that often in season."

"Season just opened," Croft said.

Janet shrugged. "I don't know. I don't hunt. I just know it's in the fall sometime."

Croft grinned. "Hell, I didn't know it either," he said. "I just checked it with the Maine cops myself."

Newman said, "Want another beer?"

"Sure," Croft said. Newman got it from the refrigerator.

"How's your Scotch, Lieutenant?"

"Fine."

Newman began to remove the dinner dishes and put them into the dishwasher. Janet finished her salad.

The two policemen were quiet for a moment.

Newman leaned his hips against the kitchen counter and said, "What do you guys want?"

Croft looked at Vincent.

Vincent smiled and sipped more Scotch. "We want to try out a hypothesis on you," he said. "Suppose there was a man who witnessed a murder and identified the killer."

Vincent paused and raised his glass and looked at the overhead light shining through the Scotch.

"And suppose then the killer leaned on this guy, or his wife, or both, and made the guy change his story. How's the guy feel, Bobby?"

"Lousy," Croft said. "He feels like he's been pushed around and made a coward, humiliated probably."

"Right. So what's he do? If he tells us, the killer will come down on him like hail on a flower, right?"

Croft said, "Right."

"So he decides to shoot the killer. That gets revenge. Takes care of his humiliation, keeps the killer from making good whatever threats he might have made, and, a plus, is sort of executing him for his crime. You know? Not just cold-blooded murder, but a kind of justice. You follow me so far?"

Newman nodded.

"You, ma'am?"

"Yes, of course," Janet said.

"But of course there's some problems. The guy's no pistolero, for one thing. And he's gotta do it so neither the cops nor the robbers know or even suspect."

"Especially the robbers," Croft said. "Cause they'll shoot him on suspicion."

"Right," Vincent said. "So this guy has to get some help and he has to find a way of doing things so no one will know."

"Especially the robbers," Croft said.

"Right," Vincent said. "Now say this guy has a friend who's a real hard-ass, excuse me, ma'am. Guy's been in the Rangers and he's had a lot of combat and he's tough enough anyway to hunt bear with a willow switch. Suppose this guy goes to his hard-ass friend and explains his problem and his friend says, hell, let's do them in, I'll help."

"That would make things a lot simpler," Croft said. "Friend might be an ex-football player, even, four, five years in the pros, something like that."

"Yeah," Vincent said, "that would be good. Now if that was the idea and then one day Karl heads up into the woods in West Overshoe, Maine, there's the chance. So this guy and his buddy, say, they head up there and they began blazing away, but the buddy gets killed and now the guy's in it alone, and there's several tough hoods against him and he pulls it off."

"And gets away," Croft said. "And comes home and keeps his mouth shut and settles back into his life."

"How's that hypothesis sound, Mr. Newman?" Vincent said.

"Bizarre," Newman said.

"Yeah," Vincent said, "that's a good word. It is bizarre. I don't believe any of it for a minute. Neither does Bobby. Right, Bobby?"

Croft said, "Right."

"Which is why I never mentioned your name to the Maine State Police," Vincent said, "or any connection you might of had with Karl, or even that you lived near Hood. Far as the State of Maine knows, you don't exist."

"So," Croft said, "if our hypothesis wasn't so crazy, you might say you are clean. Except, of course, you are clean because you never could have done something like that."

Newman didn't speak.

"In a way it's too bad," Vincent said. "I wish you were the guy in my hypothesis, because if you were I could shake your hand"—Vincent put his hand out to Newman. Newman took it—"like this and say I think you're a hell of a man."

Newman shook Vincent's hand. He said, "Hypothetically speaking, Lieutenant, shake her hand too."

Vincent stood up and shook hands with Janet. "Thanks for the Scotch," he said.

He and Croft went out to their car. Vincent got in the passenger side. Croft walked around to the driver's side and opened the door to get in. With one foot in the car he looked back at Janet and Aaron Newman standing together at their back door. He raised his right fist and held it above his shoulder for a moment. Then he got in the car and drove away.